With a deep sigh, Dominic leant back against the squabs and shut his eyes. Without the slightest difficulty he conjured up the vision of a pair of big hazel eyes, so brilliant they seemed to flash with gold fire. His doubts were gone. All consideration of age and station had long since fallen away, discarded as irrelevant in the face of his desire. He wanted Georgiana Hartley. And he intended to have her.

Stephanie Laurens

Impetuous Innocent

MIRA

ISBN 1-55166-661-8

IMPETUOUS INNOCENT

Copyright © 1994 by Stephanie Laurens.

Visit us at www.mirabooks.com

Printed in U.S.A.

Impetuous Innocent

CHAPTER ONE

"GEORGIE? GEORGIE! Open this door! Aw—c'mon, Georgie. Jus' a bit of a kiss an' cuddle. D'you hear me, Georgie? Lemme in!"

Georgiana Hartley sat cross-legged in the middle of her bed, fully clothed, a small, slight figure in the huge four-poster. The flickering light of a single candle gleamed on her guinea-gold curls, still dressed in an elegant knot. Her large hazel eyes, fixed on the door of her chamber, held an expression of annoyance; her soft lips were compressed into a disapproving line. Charles was becoming a definite boor.

It was her seventh night in England, her fourth at the Place, seat of her forefathers and home of her cousin Charles. And it was the third night she had had to seek the safety of her bedchamber at a ridiculously early hour, to avoid Charles's drink-driven importunities.

She had done it again.

Pulling a pillow across her lap, and wrinkling her nose at the musty smell that arose when she settled her elbows on it, Georgiana berated herself, for what was certainly not the first time and would undoutedly not be the last, for her apparently innate impulsiveness. It had been that alone which had driven her to leave the sunny climes of the Italian coast and return to the land of her birth. Still, on her father's death, it had seemed the most sensible course. With a deep sigh she dropped her chin on to her hands, keeping her eyes trained on the door. All was quiet, but she knew Charles was still there, just outside, hoping she might be silly enough to try to slip out.

James Hartley, painter and vivant, had left his only child to the guardianship of his only brother, her uncle Ernest. Uncle Ernest had lived at the Place. Unfortunately, he had died one month before his brother. Georgiana sniffed. Doubtless she should feel something for her uncle, but it was hard to feel grief on the death of someone you had never met—particularly when still coping with a far more shattering loss. And particularly when circumstances had conspired to land her in Charles's lap. For the news of her uncle's death had not reached James Hartley's Italian solicitors in time to stop her instinctive flight from the beauties of Ravello, her home for the last twelve years, now filled with too many painful memories. She had arrived at the Place to find Charles—Uncle Ernest's son, and a stranger to her—in possession.

The solid oak door rattled and jumped in its frame. Georgiana eyed it with increasing concern. The worn lock and the old iron hinges were all that stood between her and her drink-sodden cousin.

"Aw, Georgie, don' be a prude. You'll like't, I promise. Just a bit o' fun." A loud hiccup reached Georgiana's ears. "It's all right. You know I'll marry you. Lemme in and we'll be married tomorrow. You hear me, Georgie? C'mon, Georgie, open this door, I say!''

Georgiana sternly repressed a shiver of pure revulsion. Marry Charles? Feeling panic stir, she determinedly pushed the horrifying thought aside. Now was no time to go to pieces.

The door bounced, reverberating on its hinges as Charles made a determined assault on the thick panels. Georgiana's eyes grew round. As the thumping continued, she scanned the room for some implement, some weapon. But there was nothing, not even a candelabrum. With a grimace of resignation, she returned her gaze to the heavy oak door, philosophically waiting for whatever came next, confident that, one way or another, she would deal with it.

But the door stood firm. With one last defeated thump, Charles stopped his hammering.

"Damn you, Georgie! You won't get away! You can't escape me. You'll see—you'll have to give in, soon or late.'' A jeering, drunken laugh crept into the room. "You'll see.''

Unsteady footsteps retreated down the passage as Charles took himself off to bed, giggling crazily.

Slowly Georgiana raised her brows. She remained perched on the bed, listening. When five minutes had passed with no sound from beyond her door, she hurled aside the pillow and slipped from the bed. A determined frown settled across her heart-shaped face. She fell to pacing the room. Can't escape?

For five minutes she walked the unpolished boards. The wind whistled and moaned, little blasts worming their way through the ill-fitting shutters to send the curtains skittering. Absent-mindedly Georgiana dragged the patched quilt from the bed and flung it about her shoulders. She reviewed her options. There weren't many. She knew no one in England, had no one to turn to. But one thing was certain—she could not stay here. If she did, Charles would force her to marry him—by hook or by crook. She couldn't hide behind locked doors forever.

With the dogged and purposeful air which had carried her across an unstable Continent unharmed, she threw off the quilt and crossed to the wardrobe. Setting the door wide, she struggled to pull her trunk free. Once she got it to the floor, she tugged the cumbersome corded box to the side of the bed. She opened the heavy lid and propped it against the bed.

A scratching at the door startled her.

Slowly Georgiana straightened and eyed the scarred oak panels with misgiving.

The noise came again.

"Miss Georgie? It's me, Cruickshank."

Georgiana let out the breath she had been holding and went to the door. It was a fight to turn the heavy key. After much tugging, the bolt fell back and she eased the heavy door open. "Cruckers! Thank goodness you've come. I was racking my brains to think of how to get hold of you."

Maria Cruickshank, a thin, weedy woman, tall and lanky, with iron-grey hair tightly confined, sniffed loudly. Originally maid to Georgiana's mother, she was the closest thing to a family retainer Georgiana had.

"As if I'd not come running with all that racket. He

may be your cousin, but that Charles is no good. I told you so. *Now* do you believe me?''

Together they pushed the door shut. Cruickshank wrestled the lock home and turned to face the child-cum-lovely young woman she adored. She placed her hands on her hips and frowned grimly. ''Now, Miss Georgie, I hope you're convinced. We've got to leave this house. It's no place for the likes of you, what with Master Charles as he is. It's not what your father intended, dear me, no!''

Georgiana smiled and turned back to the bed.

Cruickshank's eyes widened. She drew full breath, girding her loins for battle. Then she saw the trunk. Her breath came out with a soft whistle. ''Ah.''

Georgiana's smile grew. ''Precisely. We're leaving. Come and help.''

Cruickshank needed no further urging. Ten minutes later, all of Georgiana's possessions were back in her trunk. While Cruickshank tightened the straps, Georgiana sat on the lid, biting the tip of one rosy finger and plotting her escape.

''Now, Cruckers, there's no point in setting out before dawn, so we may as well get some sleep. I'll stay here, and you go back downstairs and warn Ben. Charles must be dead to the world by now. I'm sure I'll be safe enough.''

Georgiana waited for the inevitable protest. Instead, Cruickshank merely snorted and clambered to her feet.

''True enough. A whole decanter of brandy he poured down his gullet. I doubt he'll be up betimes.''

Georgiana's hazel eyes widened in awe. ''Truly? Heavens!'' She wriggled her toes, then jumped to the ground. "Well, that's all the better. The longer he sleeps, the farther we'll get before he finds out."

Cruickshank sniffed disparagingly. "D'you think he'll follow?"

A worried frown drew down Georgiana's fine brows. "I really don't know. He says he's my guardian, but I don't see how that can be." She sank on to the bed, one hand brushing gold curls from her forehead in a gesture of bewilderment. "It's all so confusing."

Her tone brought Cruickshank to her side, one large hand coming up to pat Georgiana's shoulder comfortingly. "Never you worry, Miss Georgie. Ben and me, we'll see you safe."

Fleetingly, Georgiana smiled, her hand rising to grip that of her maid. "Yes, of course. I don't know what I'd have done without my two watchdogs."

Bright hazel eyes met faded blue, and Cruickshank's stern features softened. "Now, lovey, do you have any notion where you should go?"

It was the question Georgiana had spent the last three days pondering. To no avail. But her tone was determined and decisive when she said, "I've thought and thought, but I can't think of anyone. As far as I can see, the best thing I can do is throw myself on the mercy of one of the ladies of the neighbourhood. There must be someone about who remembers Uncle Ernest or Papa and will at least advise me."

Cruickshank grimaced, but did not argue the point. "I'll be back before first light. I'll bring Ben for the trunk. You get some rest now. Enough excitement for one night, you've had."

Obediently Georgiana allowed Cruickshank to help her into her nightgown, then clambered into the big bed. Cruickshank resettled the quilt and tucked the sheets under the lumpy mattress. Again the maid sniffed disparagingly.

"Even if 'twas your grandpa's house, miss, all I can say is the accommodation leaves much to be desired." With a haughty glance at the aged bedclothes, Cruickshank clumped to the door. "Just to be on the safe side, I'll lock you in."

With the problem of Charles already behind her, and her immediate actions decided, Georgiana's mind slowed. With a sigh, she snuggled deeper into the mattress and curled up tight against the cold. Her lids were already drooping as she watched the door close behind the faithful Cruickshank. The lock fell heavily into place. Georgiana yawned widely and blew out her candle.

"SHHH!" Cruickshank held a finger to her lips and with her other hand indicated a door giving off the dimly lit passage.

Georgiana nodded her understanding and slipped silently past the room where Charles's slatternly housekeeper and her equally slovenly spouse snored in drunken unison. The Pringates were new to the Place, and Georgiana could not conceive how Charles had come to hire them. They seemed to know little to nothing of managing a household. None of the old servants had remained after her uncle's death. Presumably it was hard to get good help in the country. And, even to her untutored eyes, the Place was in sorry condition, hardly an attractive proposition to experienced staff.

Mentally shrugging, she hurried on. The dank corridor ended in a huge stone-flagged kitchen. Cruickshank was struggling with the heavy back door. As she eased it open, the tell-tale sound of a horse whickering drifted in with the wet mist. Galvanised, Georgiana hurried out into the yard, Cruickshank close behind.

Her own travelling carriage, battered and worn after the long journey from Italy, but thankfully still serviceable, stood in the muddy yard, her two powerful carriage horses hitched in their harness. She spared the time to bestow a fond pat on each great grey head before allowing Ben to help her into the coach.

As the door shut, sealing her within, with Cruickshank on the seat opposite, Georgiana settled herself on the padded leather with a weary sigh. She had hoped to enjoy a rest after the jolting roads of the Continent. True, the English roads were in much better condition, but she had looked forward to keeping her feet on firm ground and her bottom on softer seats for some time. Fate, however, had clearly decided otherwise.

The carriage rocked as Ben climbed to his perch. Without his customary whistle, he set the team moving. The coach rumbled quietly out of the yard and turned into the lane.

As the miles fell slowly behind them, Georgiana wondered anew at the oddity of the Place. The old house stood in its own extensive grounds, overgrown and choked with weeds, amid fields and meadows, all lying fallow as far as she had seen. She lifted the window flap and peered through the early morning gloom. There was no sign of livestock anywhere. Fences were broken and gates hung crazily on ruptured hinges. An air of decay hung like a pall across the estate. Heaven knew, it wasn't all that large as estates went. But the Place had hit hard times, and neglect had taken its toll. She was sure her father had not known the state of his family's property. If he had, he would never have suggested she seek refuge there. Or, alternatively, he would have made some provision to restore the Place to its former glory.

As the carriage drew to the crest of a hill which marked the limit of the estate, Georgiana, leaning past the leather flap, caught a last glimpse of the grey roofs of the Place. Then the horses started on the downward slope and trees blocked her view. In truth, from what she had seen in her three days there, she doubted the Place was worth saving.

Her only regret in leaving was that she had failed to unearth the set of paintings her father had told her he had left there. Close to twenty finished canvases, he had said. The only one she was really interested in was a portrait of her mother which he had painted shortly after their marriage. He had always maintained it was the best of the handful of portraits he had done of his wife. Georgiana had looked forward to seeing again the face of her gentle mother, otherwise no more than a misty memory. But Charles had denied all knowledge of the paintings, and her surreptitious searches had failed to find any trace of them. Now, as she didn't fancy staying within Charles's reach, the paintings would remain lost to her. Philosophically, she sighed. She knew she'd made the right choice. But she had so wanted that portrait of her mother.

The lane which led to the Place was long and winding. It followed a strange line, around the boundaries of the holdings of a neighbouring estate, eventually joining a road which ultimately led to Steeple Claydon. The morning mists were lifting by the time the coach trundled into the small village of Alton Rise, no more than a cluster of cottages nestling at the first crossroads. Ben pulled the horses up before the tiny inn. He jumped down from his perch and came to the carriage window.

Georgiana pushed aside the window flap and leant out. "Can you ask where the nearest magistrate lives? If that sounds too far, ask for the nearest big landowner."

Ben nodded and disappeared into the inn. Ten minutes later he was back. "They said best to go on up to Candlewick Hall. It's owned by a London swell, name of Lord Alton. His family's been hereabouts for generations, so it seems a safe bet. The innkeeper's missus thought you'd be safe enough asking for help there."

"Heavens, Ben!" Georgiana looked at her faithful henchman in horror. "You didn't tell them about...?"

Ben shrugged his old shoulders. "'Tweren't no news to them. By all accounts, that cousin of yourn's not much liked."

Georgiana considered this view. It was not hard to believe. Charles, in three days, had proved his colours beyond question. "How far is it to Candlewick Hall?"

"No more'n a couple of miles," said Ben, hauling himself up.

As the coach lumbered forward, Georgiana sat back and rehearsed her explanation. Doubtless she would have to be frank with Lady Alton. She was not sure what she expected her ladyship to do for her. Still, at the very least, surely Lady Alton would be able to recommend a hotel in London where she could safely stay?

The coach had picked up speed on the better-surfaced road. Georgiana's wandering attention was reclaimed by the slowing of the vehicle as Ben turned the horses sharply to the left. Drawing closer to the window, she rolled up the flap and fastened it above the frame so she could gaze unimpeded at the landscape. And a very different landscape it was. In just a few miles, all evidence of rot had vanished. The fields they now passed were well tended; sheep and cattle dotted the pastures. All was neat and pleasant perfection. As if to give its blessing, the sun struck through the clouds, bathing the scene in warmth and brightness.

Georgiana was even more impressed when they reached the park of Candlewick Hall. Two stone eagles, perched atop tall gateposts, stood guard. Between them, massive wrought-iron gates hung wide. A neat gravelled drive led onwards, curving away between two lines of beech trees. The horses appreciated the even surface and trotted easily onward. Georgiana looked about her and was pleased to approve. This was how she had imagined an English gentleman's country residence would look, with trimmed shrubberies and manicured lawns falling away on one side to an ornamental lake, a white summer-house perched on an island in the middle. The vista had about it an air of peace and tranquillity. As the coach swept around a bend, she caught a glimpse of colour through the green of the trees—presumably the gardens, which meant the house was near. She scooted to the other side of the coach and looked out.

Her eyes grew round and her lips formed an "Oh" of delight.

Candlewick Hall rose before her, its cream stone walls touched here and there with bright creeper. Three storeys of square-paned windows looked down on the gravel court before the front steps. In the morning light, the house was cloaked in a still serenity, a peaceful solidity, which tugged oddly at her. Candlewick Hall embodied everything she had come back to England to find.

The pace of the coach was checked, and they rocked to a stop before the white steps leading up to two massive front doors. Ben swung down and came to assist her to alight. He escorted her up the steps and plied the heavy knocker.

Georgiana faced the heavy wooden doors. It had seemed much easier to claim help from an unknown lady when she had been sitting in her bed last night. But the memory of Charles's ravings stiffened her resolve. As the sound of footsteps drew nearer, she took a deep breath and fixed a confident smile on her lips.

"Yes?"

A stately butler looked majestically down upon her.

"Good morning. My name is Georgiana Hartley. I wonder if I might have a word with Lady Alton?"

Georgiana was pleased with her tone. She sounded confident and in control, despite the fact she was inwardly quaking. If the butler was this starchy, what was his mistress like? She kept her chin up and waited.

The butler did not move. Georgiana felt her confidence draining, dissipating like the morning mist under the intensity of his scrutiny. She wondered if the man was hard of hearing, and was gathering her courage to repeat her request in more strident tones when he smiled, quite kindly, and bowed. "If you will step into the drawing-room, Miss Hartley, I will inform Lord Alton immediately."

Buoyed by her success, Georgiana was across the threshold before she analysed his words. She came to an abrupt halt. "Oh! But it was Lady Alton I wished to see."

"Yes, of course, miss. If you would take a seat?"

Unable to resist the deferential and strangely compelling courtesy of the impeccable butler, Georgiana found herself ushered into a beautifully appointed room and made comfortable in a wing-chair. Having ascertained that she was not in need of any refreshment thus early in the day, the dignified personage withdrew.

Feeling slightly dazed, Georgiana looked about her. The interior of Candlewick Hall did justice to its exterior. Exquisite taste and a judicious eye had chosen and arranged all the furnishings, creating and enhancing a mood of peace and serenity to match that of the gardens. Her hazel gaze wandered over the room, coming to rest on the large painting in pride of place above the mantelpiece. As a painter's daughter, she could not do otherwise than admire Fragonard. She was intrigued, nevertheless, to find a picture incorporating numerous naked female forms so publicly displayed. A more private room would, she thought, have been more appropriate. But then, she reminded herself, she knew nothing of the latest whims of English social taste. And there was no doubt the Fragonard was an exquisite work of art.

The subtle colours of the room slowly eased her tension, seeping into her sight and mind. Georgiana smiled to herself and settled back in the chair. Candlewick Hall seemed designed to calm the senses. With a grateful sigh, she relaxed.

The effects of three late nights dragged at her eyelids. She would close them. Just for a moment.

"THERE'S A YOUNG LADY to see you, m'lord."

Dominic Ridgeley, fifth Viscount Alton, lifted his blue eyes to his butler's face. Around him, on the polished mahogany table, the remains of a substantial breakfast bore mute testimony to his recent occupation. But the dishes had been pushed aside to make way for a pile of letters, one of which his lordship clasped in one long-fingered hand.

"I beg your pardon?"

"A young lady has called, m'lord." Not a quiver of emotion showed on the butler's lined face.

Lord Alton's black brows rose. His features became perceptibly harder, his blue gaze perceptibly chillier. "Have you taken leave of your senses, Duckett?"

Such a question, in such a tone, would have reduced most servants to incoherent gibbering. But Duckett was a butler of the highest standing. And he had known the present Lord Alton from the cradle. He answered the question with an infinitesimal smile. "Naturally not, m'lord."

His answer appeared to appease his master. Lord Alton regarded his henchman with a puzzled and slightly wary frown. "Oh?"

At the prompt, Duckett explained. "It seems the young lady requires assistance with some difficulty, m'lord. She asked to see Lady Alton. She appears to be in some distress. I thought it wise not to turn her away. Her name is Miss Hartley."

"Hartley?" The black brows drew down. "But there aren't any Miss Hartleys at the Place, are there?"

In response to his master's quizzical look, Duckett graciously informed him, "I have heard that Mr James Hartley's daughter has been visiting the Place for the past few days. From the Continent, I believe."

"Staying with frightful Charles? Poor girl."

"Exactly so, m'lord."

Lord Alton fixed Duckett with a suspicious look. "You said she was distressed. She's not weeping and having the vapours, is she?"

"Oh, no, m'lord. Miss Hartley is perfectly composed."

Lord Alton frowned again. "Then how do you know she's distressed?"

Duckett coloured slightly. "It was her hands, m'lord. She was clutching her reticule so tightly, her knuckles were quite white."

Suitably impressed by his butler's astuteness, Lord Alton leant back in his chair, absent-mindedly laying the letter he had been reading on the pile before him. Then he glanced up. "You think I should see her?"

Duckett met his master's eye and did not misunderstand his question. No one who was acquainted with Lord Alton could fail to comprehend the delicacy of the matter. For a young lady to meet a gentleman alone, particularly in the gentleman's house, with no other lady anywhere about, was hardly the sort of behaviour someone as conservative as Duckett would normally encourage. And when the gentleman in question was Lord Dominic Alton, the situation took on an even more questionable hue. But Duckett's perception was acute. Miss Hartley was in trouble and out of her depth. His master could be relied upon to provide the answer to her troubles. And, regardless of his reputation, she stood in no danger from him. She was too young and too green, not his type at all. So, Duckett cleared his throat and said, "Despite the—er—conventions, yes, m'lord, I think you should see her."

With a sigh, Lord Alton rose, stretching to his full six feet. Relaxing, he shook out his cuffs and settled his dark blue coat over his broad shoulders. Then he looked up and wagged an admonitory finger at Duckett. "If this lands me in scandal, old friend, it'll be all your fault."

Duckett grinned and opened the door for his master. "As you wish, m'lord. She's in the drawing-room."

With one last warning glance, Lord Alton passed through the door and crossed the hall.

GEORGIANA'S DREAM was distinctly disturbing. In it, she had transformed into one of the nymphs depicted in the Fragonard canvas. Together with her unknown sisters, she cavorted freely through a sylvan glade, blushing at the cool drift of the breeze across her naked skin. Abruptly, she halted. Someone was watching her. She glanced around, blushing even more rosily. But there was no one in sight. The sensation of being watched grew. She opened her eyes.

And gazed bemusedly into eyes of cerulean blue.

Her gaze widened, and she saw the man behind the eyes. She stopped breathing, no longer sure which was reality and which the dream. For the man watching her, a gleam of undisguised appreciation in the depths of those beautiful blue eyes, was undoubtedly a god. And even more disturbing than her erotic dream. His shoulders were broad, filling her sight, his body long and lean and muscular. His face was strongly featured, yet held the clean lines painters adored. Thick dark hair cloaked his head in elegant waves, softening the effect of his determinedly squared chin. Finely drawn lips held the hint of a disturbing smile. And his eyes, glorious blue, set under strongly arched brows and framed by lashes too long and thick for a man, seemed to hold all the promise of a summer's afternoon.

"Oh!" It was the most coherent response she could muster.

The vision smiled. Georgiana's heart lurched.

"You were sleeping so peacefully I was loath to disturb you."

The deep tones of his voice enclosed Georgiana in a warmth reminiscent of fine velvet. With an effort, she straightened, forcing her body to behave and her mind to function. "I... I'm so sorry. I must have drifted off. I was waiting for Lady Alton."

The gentleman retreated slightly to lean one elegant arm along the mantelpiece, one booted foot resting on the hearth. The blue eyes, disconcertingly, remained trained on her face.

"I'm desolated to disappoint you." The smile that went with the words said otherwise. "Allow me to introduce myself. Lord Dominic Alton, entirely at your service."

He swept her an elegant bow, blue eyes gleaming.

"But alas, I've yet to marry. There is, therefore, no Lady Alton."

"Oh, *how* unfortunate!"

The anguished assessment surprised Dominic. He was not used to such a response from personable young women. His lips twitched and his eyes came alight with unholy amusement. "Quite!"

His tone brought the hazel gaze to his face. But she showed no consciousness of her phrasing. Seeing real consternation in the warm hazel eyes, Dominic rejected the appealing idea of explaining it to her. Clearly, Duckett's assessment of her state was accurate. She might be sitting calmly, rather than indulging in hysterics, as females were so lamentably prone to do, but he had no doubt she was seriously adrift and knew not which way to turn. The expression in her wide hazel eyes said so. In response, he smiled beguilingly. "But I gather you have some problem. Perhaps I could be of help?"

His polite query flustered Georgiana. How could she explain…? To a man…?

"Er—I don't think…" She rose, clutching her reticule tightly. As she did so, her gaze went beyond Lord Alton to the Fragonard. Georgiana froze. What sort of man, with no wife, hung a scandalous masterpiece in his drawing-room? The answer threatened to scuttle what wits she still possessed.

Unknown to Georgiana, her thoughts passed clearly across her face, perfectly readable to the accomplished gentleman watching her. All Dominic's experience told him to accept her withdrawal as the blessed release it doubtless was. But some whimsical and unexpected impulse pushed him to learn what strange story, what quirk of fate, was responsible for depositing such a very delightful morsel on his doorstep. Besides, he didn't entirely like her assumption that he was powerless to help her. He drew himself to his full height and fixed her with a stern eye. "My dear Miss Hartley, I do hope you're not about to say you '—doubt that I can be of assistance—' before you've even told me the problem."

Georgiana blinked. She had, of course, been about to say just that. With the ground cut from under her feet, she struggled to find some acceptable way out.

Lord Alton was smiling again. Strange, she had never before encountered a smile that warmed her as his did.

"Please sit down, Miss Hartley. Can I get you some refreshment? No? Well, then, why don't you just tell me what your problem is? I promise you, I don't shock easily."

Georgiana glanced up, but the blue eyes were innocent. Sinking once more into the wing-chair, she considered her choices. If she insisted on leaving Lord Alton without asking for his advice, where would she go? And, more importantly, how far behind her was Charles? That thought, more than any other, drove her to speak. "I really wanted to ask for some advice…on what I should do, finding myself in the situation I… I now find myself in." She paused, wondering how detailed her explanation need be.

"Which is?" came the soft prompt.

The need to confide in someone was strong. Mentally shrugging, Georgiana threw caution to the winds. "I recently returned to England from the Continent. I've lived for the last twelve years in Italy with my father, James Hartley. He died a few months ago, leaving me to the guardianship of my uncle, Ernest Hartley."

She looked up. Lord Alton's expression was sympathetic. He nodded encouragingly. Drawing a deep breath, she continued. "I returned to England immediately. I…didn't wish to remain in Italy. On my arrival at Hartley Place, I learnt that my uncle had died a month or so before my father. My cousin Charles owns the Place now." Georgiana hesitated.

"I'm slightly acquainted with Charles Hartley, if that's any help. I might add that I would not consider him a fit person for a young lady such as yourself to share a roof with."

His cool, impersonal tone brought a blush to Georgiana's cheek.

Seeing it, Dominic knew he had struck close to the truth.

Keeping her eyes fixed on the empty fireplace, Georgiana struggled on. "I'm afraid…that is to say, Charles seems to have developed a fixation. In short," she continued, desperation lending her words, "he has been trying to force me to marry him. I left the house this morning, very early."

She glanced up and, to her surprise, found no difficulty in meeting his lordship's blue gaze. "I've no one in England I can turn to, my lord. I was hoping to ask your wife for advice as to what I should do."

Dominic's gaze rested on the heart-shaped face and large honey-gold eyes turned so trustingly towards him. For some perverse reason, he knew he was going to help her. Ignoring the inner voice which whispered he was mad even to contemplate such a thing, he asked, "Have you any particular course of action in mind?"

"Well, I did think of going to London. I thought perhaps I could become a companion to some lady."

Dominic forcibly repressed a shudder. Such a glorious creature would have no luck in finding that sort of employment. She was flexing her fingers, her attention momentarily distracted. His eyes slid gently over her figure. The grey dress she wore fitted well, outlining a pair of enticingly sweet breasts, young and firm and high. Her skin was perfect—peaches and cream. As she was seated, he had no way of judging her legs, although, by the evidence of her slender feet, he suspected they would prove to be long and slim. Her waist was hidden by the fall of her dress, but the swell of her hips was unmistakable. If Georgiana Hartley became stranded in London, he could guess where she'd end. Which, all things considered, would be a great shame. Her candid gaze returned to his face.

"I have my own maid and coachman. I thought that might help."

Help? A companion with her own maid and coachman? Dominic managed to keep his face impassive. There was no point in telling her how ludicrous her ideas were, for she wasn't going to hire out as a companion. Not if he had anything to say in the matter. The wretched life most paid companions led, neither servant nor family, stranded in limbo between stairs, was not for Miss Hartley.

"I will have to think of what's best to be done. Instant solutions are likely to come unstuck. I've always found it much more useful to consider carefully before committing any irrevocable act."

Listen to yourself! screamed his inner voice.

Dominic smiled sweetly. "I suggest you spend an hour or so with my housekeeper, while I consider the alternatives." The smile broadened. "Believe me, there are alternatives."

Georgiana blinked. She wasn't sure what to make of that. She hoped she hadn't jumped from the frying-pan into the fire. But he was turning her over to the care of his housekeeper, which hardly fitted with the image revolving in her mind. There was another problem. "Charles might follow me."

"I can assure you this is one place Charles will never look. And I doubt he'd pursue you to London. You're perfectly safe here." Dominic turned and tugged the bell-pull. Then he swung back to face Georgiana and smiled reassuringly. "Charles and I don't exactly get on, you see."

A pause ensued. While Miss Hartley studied her hands, Dominic studied Miss Hartley. She was a sweetly turned piece, but too gentle and demure for his taste. A damsel in distress—Duckett had been right there. Clearly, it behoved him to help her. The cost would be negligible; it would hardly take up much of his time and might even afford him some amusement. Aside from anything else, it would presumably annoy Charles Hartley, and that was a good enough reason in itself. He determinedly quashed his inner voice, that advocate of self-protection at all costs, and returned to his agreeable contemplation of Miss Hartley.

The door opened, and Georgiana came slowly to her feet.

"My lord?"

Dominic turned. "Duckett, please ask Mrs Landy to attend us."

"Yes, m'lord." Duckett bowed himself from the room, a smile of quiet satisfaction on his face.

AFTER A PLEASANT and reassuring hour spent with Mrs Landy, Georgiana was conducted back to the drawing-room. The motherly housekeeper had been shocked to learn of Georgiana's plight and even more moved when she discovered she had missed her breakfast. Now, fortified with muffins and jam and steaming coffee, and having been assured her two servants had been similarly supplied, Georgiana faced the prospect of her interview with Lord Alton with renewed confidence. No gentleman who possessed a housekeeper like Mrs Landy could be a villain.

She smiled sweetly at the butler, who seemed much less intimidating now, and passed through the door he held open for her. Lord Alton was standing by the fireplace. He looked up as she entered, and smiled. Georgiana was struck anew by his handsomeness and the subtle aura of a deeper attractiveness that owed nothing to his elegant attire, but derived more from the quality of his smile and the lights that danced in those wonderful eyes.

He inclined his head politely in response to her curtsy and, still smiling, waved her to the wing-chair. Georgiana seated herself and settled her skirts, thankful she had this morning donned one of her more modish gowns, a grey kerseymere with a fine white linen fichu, edged with expensive Italian lace. Comfortable, she raised expectant eyes to his lordship's darkbrowed face.

For a full minute, he seemed to be looking at her and thinking of something else. Then, abruptly, he cleared his throat.

"How old are you, Miss Hartley?"

Georgiana answered readily, assuming him to be considering what employment might best suit her years. "Eighteen, my lord."

Eighteen. Good. He was thirty-two. She was too young, thank God. It must just be his gentlemanly instincts that were driving him to help her. At thirty-two, one was surely beyond the stage of lusting after schoolroom chits. Dominic smiled his practised smile.

"In light of your years, I think you'll find it will

take some time to discover a suitable position. Such opportunities don't grow on trees, you know.'' He kept his manner determinedly avuncular. ''I've been thinking of what lady of my acquaintance would be most useful in helping you. My sister, Lady Winsmere, is often telling me she pines for distraction.'' That, at least, was the truth. If he knew Bella, she would leap at the opportunity for untold distraction that he intended to offer her in the charming person of Miss Georgiana Hartley.

Georgiana watched Lord Alton's face intently. Thus far, his measured statements made perfect sense, but his patronising tone niggled. She was hardly a child.

''I have written a letter to her,'' Dominic continued, pausing to draw a folded parchment from his coat, ''in which I've explained your predicament.'' His lips involuntarily twitched as he imagined what Bella would make of his disclosures. ''I suggest you take it and deliver it in person to Lady Winsmere in Green Street.'' He smiled into Miss Hartley's warmed honey eyes. ''Bella, despite her occasional flights of fancy, is quite remarkably sane and will know precisely how you should go on. I've asked her to supervise you in your search for employment, for you will be sadly out of touch with the way things are done. You may place complete confidence in her judgement.''

Relief swept over Georgiana. She rose and took the letter. Holding it carefully, she studied the strong black script boldly inscribed across the parchment. Her fingers moved across the thick, finely textured paper. She felt oddly reassured, as if a confidence placed had proved to be well founded. After her problems with

Charles, the world seemed to be righting itself. "My lord, I don't know how to thank you. You've been more help than I expected, certainly more than I deserve." Her soft voice sounded so small in that elegant room. She raised her eyes to his, smiling in sincere gratitude.

Unaccountably irritated, Dominic waved one fine hand dismissively. "It was nothing, I assure you. It's entirely my pleasure to be able to help you. Now one more point." He hurried on, strangely unwilling to bear more of Miss Hartley's gratitude. "It seems to me that if Charles is out there scouting about he'll be looking for your carriage, with your coachman atop. I've therefore given orders for you to be conveyed to London in one of my carriages, together with your maid. One of my coachmen will drive you and will return with the carriage. After a few days, when Charles has given up, your coachman will follow you with your coach. I trust such an arrangement is satisfactory?"

Georgiana felt slightly stunned. He seemed to have thought of everything. Efficiently, smoothly, in just one short hour he had cleared the obstacles from her path and made all seem easy. "My lord, you overwhelm me. But surely—you might need your carriage?"

"I assure you my carriage will be…better used conveying you to London than it otherwise would be," Dominic responded suavely, only just managing to avoid a more subtly flattering selection of words. God! Dealing with an innocent was trying his wits. A long time had passed since he had engaged in social discourse with a virtuous young lady of only eighteen summers. It was too abominably easy to slip into the more sophisticated and seductive modes of conversation he used almost exclusively to females these days. Which, he ruefully reminded himself, was a definite reflection on the types of ladies whose company he currently kept.

With another dazzling smile, Georgiana Hartley inclined her head in acceptance. At his intimation, she fell into step beside him, gliding towards the door on tiny, grey-slippered feet.

Still bemused, and with the feeling that events were suddenly moving rather faster than she could cope with, Georgiana could nevertheless find no fault with his arrangements.

Duckett met them in the hall with the information that the coach stood ready.

Dominic could not resist offering her his arm. With gentlemanly courtesy he conducted her to the coach, pausing while she exchanged farewells with Ben, surprising everyone, Ben included, by breaking off her words to give him a quick hug. Then Dominic handed her into the luxuriously appointed coach, wherein her maid was already installed, and stood back. Duckett shut the door firmly. The coachman, Jiggs, gave the horses the office. The coach pulled smoothly away.

Dominic Ridgeley stood on the steps of his manor house, his hands sunk in his pockets, and watched his coach roll out of sight. Then, when he could no longer see the swaying carriage roof, he turned to go inside, pausing to kick at a piece of gravel inadvertently, inexcusably resident on the steps. With a sigh and a pensive smile, as if some pleasant interlude had come to its inevitable conclusion, he went inside and shut the door.

CHAPTER TWO

NIGHT had descended by the time Lord Alton's travelling carriage drew to a halt on the cobbles before the elegant town house of Lord and Lady Winsmere. Georgiana glanced up at the tiers of lamplit windows reaching high above the street. Beside her, Cruickshank sat silent, her lips set in a severe line. The groom swung down and trotted up the steps to jangle the doorbell before returning to help them to the pavement.

A portly butler appeared. One glance at the groom's livery was apparently enough to effect instant entrance for Georgiana and Cruickshank.

Georgiana allowed the butler to remove her pelisse. Then she turned and, in a voice tinged with nervousness, said, "I wish to speak with Lady Winsmere, if you please. I have a letter of introduction from Lord Alton."

Despite the butler's gracious bow and solemn face, Georgiana was instantly aware of his avid interest.

"I will convey your letter to Lady Winsmere, miss. If you would care to wait in the drawing-room?"

Shown into a reception-room of pleasing proportions, Georgiana stopped and blinked. The door shut behind her. Cruickshank had dutifully remained in the hall. Georgiana scanned the room, then, finding nothing of greater moment to consider, gave her attention to a careful appraisal of the white and gilt décor. The room was well stocked with furniture, and every available flat surface sprouted at least one ornament. The rule seemed to be that if it wasn't white it had to be gilded. Not even the ornate cornices had escaped. The effect was overpowering. With a sigh and a shrug for English fashions, Georgiana chose a stiff-backed, spindle-legged chair, heavily gilded and upholstered in white damask, and gingerly sat down.

Her gaze roamed the walls once more, but there was no Fragonard to provide distraction.

She folded her hands in her lap and tried to subdue the uncomfortable feeling of encroaching upon those whom she had no right to call on. But Lord Alton had seemed unperturbed by her request for help. Maybe, despite her misgivings, there was nothing so very peculiar about her predicament. At least, not to an English mind. Determined to be optimstic, she endeavoured to compose herself to meet Lady Winsmere's questions. Doubtless, she would have a good few. What was she making of her brother's letter?

Only then did Georgiana realise she had no idea in what light Lord Alton had presented her to his sister. The thick parchment had been fixed with a heavy lump of red wax, on which the seal of the Viscounts Alton had been imprinted. Georgiana frowned. A wave of tiredness rose up to envelop her. Not for the first time since leaving the comfort of Candlewick Hall, she wondered at the wisdom of her actions. She was too impulsive. Often she had landed herself in the suds by rushing headlong on her fate—witness her flight from Ravello. But it was too late to draw back now. She grimaced. The more she thought of it, the more clearly she perceived her inability to influence the course of events Lord Alton had charted for her. These, presumably, would determine her immediate future. Somehow she had placed herself in Lord Alton's hands.

Georgiana stifled a despondent sigh. She hoped she looked more confident than she felt.

On the floor above, Bella, Lady Winsmere, was in the middle of her toilette, preparatory to attending the theatre. A knock on the door of her boudoir was followed by a whispered conference between her dresser, Hills, and her butler, Johnson.

Distracted from the delicate task of improving on nature, Bella frowned. "What is it, Hills?"

Her black-garbed dresser produced a folded parchment, inscribed to herself in her brother's unmistakable scrawl. Intrigued, Bella immediately laid down her haresfoot. Bits of red wax scattered in all directions as she broke open the seal.

Five short minutes later, she was crossing her front hall in a froth of lacy peignoir, rendered barely respectable by a silk wrapper. Johnson, having anticipated her impetuous descent, stood ready to open the drawing-room door for her.

As the door shut, bringing her guest to her feet, Bella's bright blue eyes, very like her brother's, surveyed her unexpected visitor.

Unconsciously clutching her reticule, once again in a tell-tale grip, Georgiana beheld an enchanting vision, fashionably slender and no taller than she herself was.

But there the resemblance ended. Lady Winsmere was dark-haired, her fine skin was alabaster-white. Her blue eyes Georgiana had seen before. And the elegance of her lacy gown made Georgiana feel awkward and abominably young.

For her part, Bella saw a girl on the threshold of womanhood. Her innocence shone beacon-clear. She was all honey and cream, from the top of her curls, tinged with the sun's kiss, to her delicately tinted complexion. Her golden eyes contained a quality of unusual candour. And she had no more inches than Bella herself. Bella's face brightened. A little sigh escaped her. With a generous and genuine smile, she floated forward, both hands outstretched to capture Georgiana's cold fingers in a warm clasp.

"My dear! So you are Georgiana Hartley! Dominic has written me all about you. You poor dear! What a dreadful thing to happen, and you newly returned to England. You must let me help you."

At Georgiana's murmured, "My lady," Bella broke her stride. But when Georgiana attempted to curtsy, Bella held on tightly to her hands, preventing it.

"No, no, my dear. You're among friends here. You must call me Bella, and I hope you won't think me terribly forward if I call you Georgiana." She tilted her small head to one side, blue eyes twinkling.

Georgiana found her engaging manners difficult to resist. "Why, of course not, my... Bella. But truly, I feel as if I'm imposing dreadfully upon you."

"Oh, pooh!" Bella pulled a face. "I'm always bored; there's so little to do in London these days. I'm positively thrilled Dominic thought to send you to me!

Why—'' she paused, struck by a wayward thought
"—just think. If you'd grown up at the Place, we
would have been neighbours.'' Bella waved Georgiana
to the chaise and sank to the white damask beside her.
"So, you see, there's no need for you to feel at all
bothered about staying with me.''

Georgiana's head reeled. "Oh! But I wouldn't
dream of imposing—''

"Not at all! It's the very thing. You have nowhere
to go and we have plenty of room.'' Bella gazed intently at Georgiana. "Truly, it's no trouble at all.''

"But—''

Bella shook her head. "No buts. Just consider it as
doing me a favour. We'll have such fun. I'll take you
about and introduce you to all the right people.''

Despite a sudden tug of impetuosity, urging acceptance of the exciting offer, Georgiana, grappling with
the flow of Bella's burgeoning plans, felt constrained
to protest. "But my la... Bella. I don't think Lord
Alton can have properly explained. I need to find a
post as a companion.''

Recalling the specific instructions contained in her
brother's letter, Bella assured Georgiana that he had,
indeed, explained fully. "But my dear, in order to find
the right post for you, particularly considering your
age, you must first become established in society.''

Bella watched the frown gathering in Georgiana's
fine eyes. Before her guest could raise any further ob-
jection, she raised one slim, restraining hand. "Now
before you start arguing—and I do so hate people who
must forever be sniping and finding fault—I must tell
you that you will be doing me the biggest favour imag-

inable in allowing me to help you. You can have no idea how boring it is to pass the Season with no real purpose. The Little Season is coming up in a few weeks. I implore you to relieve my frustrations and stay with me and allow me to present you. Surely that's not too much to ask?'' Bella's big blue eyes pleaded eloquently.

Bemused by the sudden twist the situation seemed to have taken, with Lady Winsmere now begging the favour of her company, and feeling too drained by the day's events to fight a fate so apparently desirable, Georgiana found herself weakly acquiescing. ''If it's really not too much trouble… Just until I can find a position.''

''Splendid!'' Bella grinned in delight. ''Now the first thing we must do is get you settled in a bedchamber. A hot bath is just what you need. Always so soothing after travelling.''

With a magic wave of one small bejewelled hand, Bella took charge. In short order, Georgiana, her luggage, Cruickshank, dinner on a tray and a large tub together with steaming hot water to fill it had been conveyed to the best guest chamber on the floor above.

An hour later, after she had closed the door of Georgiana's room behind her, having seen her young guest settled in bed, Bella Winsmere's face took on a pensive frown. Slowly she descended the stairs, so deep in thought that she was halfway across the hall towards the front door before she recalled her intended destination. Swinging about, she turned her steps towards the library at the back of the house.

At the sound of the door opening, Lord Winsmere

looked up from the pile of documents he was working on. His lean face lit with a smile of great warmth. He laid aside his pen to reach out a welcoming arm to his wife.

With a quick smile, Bella went to him, returning his embrace and dropping a quick kiss on his greying hair.

"I thought you were bound for Drury Lane tonight?" Lord Winsmere was more than twenty years older than his beautiful wife. His staid, sometimes regal demeanour contrasted sharply with her effervescent charm. Many had wondered why, from among her myraid suitors, Bella Ridgeley had chosen to bestow her dainty hand on a man almost old enough to be her father. But over the years society had been forced to accept the fact that the beautiful Bella was sincerely and most earnestly in love with her eminently respectable lord.

"I was, but we have an unexpected guest."

"Oh?"

His lordship pushed his papers aside, consigning them to the morrow. If his Bella had sought him out, then she had some problem to discuss. He rose and, Bella's hand still in his, led her to the two armchairs stationed before the fireplace.

Bella sat, chewing the tip of one rosy finger, a habit when thinking profoundly.

Smiling, Lord Winsmere seated himself opposite her and waited for her to begin.

"It's really most intriguing."

Inured to his spouse's methods of explanation, Lord Winsmere made no response.

Eventually Bella gathered her wandering mind and

embarked on her story. "Dominic's sent a girl to stay."

At that, Lord Winsmere's brows rose sharply. But the knowledge that, despite his apparent lack of moral concern, Dominic Ridgeley had never permitted the slightest breath of scandal to touch his sister's fair name held him silent.

"She's a would-have-been-neighbour. Her name's Georgiana Hartley. Her father was a painter, one James Hartley. He died in Italy some months ago and Georgiana was left to her uncle's care. Most unfortunately, her uncle, who lived at the Place—you know, it's that funny estate that was made by selling off a piece of Candlewick—well, he died too. Just before her father, only she didn't know that, being in Italy. The long and the short of it is, Georgiana travelled all the way from Italy, only to find her uncle dead and her cousin Charles in charge. It only needs to add that Charles is an out-and-out bounder and you have the picture." Bella spread her hands and glanced at her husband.

"How did Dominic come to be involved?"

"It seems Georgiana was forced to flee the Place at dawn this morning. She doesn't know anyone—no one at all. She asked at the Three Bells, thinking to find a sympathetic lady in residence at a neighbouring estate. Of course, the Tadlows sent her to Candlewick. You know how all our people are about Dominic."

Lord Winsmere nodded sagely, a thin smile hovering about his lips at the thought of the godlike status his far from godly brother-in-law enjoyed on his own lands.

"Well, she went to the Hall and met Duckett. And then Dominic came and persuaded her to tell him all." Bella suddenly broke off. "Oh—are you imagining she must be some encroaching mushroom?" Her ladyship leant forward slightly and fixed her big eyes on her husband. "Truly, Arthur, it is not so. She's the most engaging little thing. So innocent and green and so...so trusting."

Lord Winsmere's fine brows rose slightly.

Abruptly Bella dropped to her knees, draping her silk-clad arms over her husband's knees. She smiled, impish and seductive all at once. "Please, Arthur. Please say she may stay. You know how bored I am. She's perfectly presentable, I give you my word. I could take her about and present her to the *ton*... Oh— I'd have such fun! The balls and parties are so tame, if one's not part of the game. Please, my love. Say she may stay."

Lord Winsmere smiled down into his wife's upturned face while his mind canvassed the possibilities presented by her unknown guest. Their son and only child was ensconced in the country, happily growing out of short coats. Jonathon's constitution was not sickly but did not cope well with the stale air of the capital. But his own work necessitated his presence in London. Bella, torn between the two men in her life, had chosen to remain by his side. As he doubted he could live without her, he would willingly make any sacrifice to alleviate the boredom he knew she found in the predictable rounds of tonnish entertainment. But an unknown girl? And, if he knew his Bella, she meant to fire the chit off with all flags flying. Not that the

expense worried him. But was the girl truly as innocent as Bella, herself not much more experienced for
all her matronliness, believed?

He reached out a finger to trace the graceful curve
of his wife's brow. Impulsively, she caught his hand
and kissed it, then continued to hold it in a warm clasp,
her eyes on his face.

"You needn't worry about the cost. Dominic said
to charge everything to him."

"Did he, indeed? How very magnanimous, to be
sure." Lord Winsmere's mobile lips twitched. Dominic Ridgeley had inherited a fortune of sizeable proportions and could easily afford to underwrite the
launching of an unknown damsel into the *ton.* The
question that exercised Lord Winsmere's mind was
why his hedonistic brother-in-law should wish to do
such a peculiar thing.

"I think perhaps I should meet this paragon before
I allow you to take her under your wing."

Bella's eyes grew round. "Are you thinking she is
one of Dominic's paramours? I must admit, I did, too,
at first. Well, whoever would imagine him having any
contact with an innocent young girl? But I assure you
she's just what Dominic says—young and innocent
and...and hopelessly lost. I dare say she'll have no
idea how to go on, having lived in Italy all this time."

Lord Winsmere's face remained impassive. The
possibility that his brother-in-law had sent Bella a lady
needing help to cover some lapse of acceptable conduct had certainly occurred, only to be immediately
dismissed. Few knew better than himself that, despite
Viscount Alton's reputation as a well heeled, insidi-

ously charming and potentially dangerous rake, underneath, Dominic Ridgeley adhered most assiduously to a code of conduct that, if it were more widely recognised, would see him hailed as a pillar of society. But it was the veneer society saw—a façade erected to hide the boredom of a man who had never had to exert himself to win any prize. Born with the proverbial silver spoon tightly clamped between his jaws, and with the compounding assets of a handsome face and an athletic frame, there was little Dominic Ridgeley needed in life. And what he did want came easily. Society adored him. His well born mistresses fell at his feet. With ready charm, Dominic moved through it all, and with the years his boredom grew.

"What, exactly, did Dominic say?"

Bella smiled and shifted to sit at his feet, her hand still holding his, her shining blue eyes turned lovingly on him. "Well..."

Fifteen minutes later, Lord Winsmere felt he was in possession of all the salient facts. The only puzzle remaining was his brother-in-law's motives. A whimsical start? Dominic was hardly in his dotage. Nevertheless, young and girlish and innocent was assuredly not his style. The spectre of Elaine, Lady Changley drifted into Lord Winsmere's mind. Involuntarily, his face assumed an expression of distaste. Lady Changley was definitely not young and girlish, and not by the remotest stretch of the most pliable imagination could she be described as innocent.

Bella saw the disapprobation in her husband's face. Her own face fell. "You don't like the idea?"

Recalled, Lord Winsmere smiled and confessed, "I

was thinking of something else.'' At his wife's fond smile, he continued, ''If the girl is all you and Dominic seem to think, I have no objections to your taking her under your wing. Aside from anything else, she'll have to be terribly innocent to swallow this yarn of yours about the way to securing a position being to make a splash in society.''

Bella met his sceptical look with a bright grin. ''Oh, I'll manage it—you'll see.''

Five minutes later Lord Winsmere returned to his desk to tidy his papers away for the night. The memory of Bella's bright eyes remained with him. She was more animated than she had been in months. Perhaps Dominic's damsel in distress was an angel in disguise. He smiled fondly. All in all, he was looking forward to meeting his wife's protégée.

THE SHARP CALL of the orange sellers woke Georgiana. Bemused, she stared about her, then remembered where she was and how she came to be there. Despite the evidence of her eyes, reality retained the aura of a dream. She was lying propped in her pillows, still wondering, when Cruickshank came bustling through the door with her early morning chocolate.

Georgiana waited silently for her maid's comment. No one could size up an establishment faster or more accurately than Cruickshank.

No sniffs were forthcoming. Not even a snort.

As she accepted the tray across her knees, Georgiana was taken aback to hear the dour maid humming.

Catching sight of her mistress's startled look, Cruickshank smiled. ''A right proper place they keep here, Miss Georgie. No need to teach them anything. Mrs Biggins, the housekeeper, is a tight old bird, but fair, mark my words. Runs the place just as she should. And Johnson—he's the butler—and her ladyship's dresser, Hills, are everything they ought to be. A relief, it is, after the Place.''

''So you're comfortable here?''

At the wardrobe, Cruickshank nodded emphatically. She drew out a violet morning gown trimmed with fine lace and laid it ready across a chair, then went to search for the accessories.

Georgiana sipped her chocolate. As the sweet warmth slid down her throat and heat seeped through her body, she sighed. So wonderful—to have real chocolate again. She closed her eyes and was immediately back on the terrace at Ravello, her father opposite, across the breakfast-table. Abruptly she opened her eyes, blinking rapidly. Enough of that! She had shed all the tears she possessed long ago. Her father had wanted her to get on with her life. He had warned her not to grieve for him. He had had a good life, so he had said, and wanted his daughter to have the same. That was why she was to return to England and the bosom of her family. Some bosom Charles had turned out to be. At the thought, Georgiana wriggled her toes. The idea of Charles scouring the countryside for her, only to return, dusty and beaten, to the damp and musty Place, brought a glow of satisfaction to her honey-gold eyes. Serve him right.

''How long are we staying here?''

Cruickshank came to draw back the covers. Georgiana slid from the bed, busying herself with washing

48   IMPETUOUS INNOCENT

and dressing while she considered how best to answer.
She had not discussed her plan to get a position with
either of her servants, sure they would veto the idea
as soon as they heard it. Come what may, she was
determined to keep them with her. They were all that
remained of her parents' happy household.

So, standing patiently as Cruickshank laced her
gown, she answered airily, "I'll have to discuss the
matter with Lady Wins… Bella. She seems to wish us
to stay for a while."

Cruickshank snorted. "So I gathered. Still, she
seems a real lady; none of your hoity-toity airs about
that one."

Georgiana grinned, remembering Bella's fussing the
night before. It had been a long time since anyone
other than Cruickshank had fussed over her.

After Cruickshank had settled her curls in a knot on
the top of her head, Georgiana tentatively made her
way downstairs. Johnson found her in the front hall
and, gracious as ever, directed her to the breakfast parlour overlooking the rear gardens.

"There you are, my dear!"

Georgiana had the feeling Bella had been waiting
for her to appear. Her hostess surged across the Turkey
carpet in a cloud of fine-figured muslin. Georgiana returned her smile.

"Are you sure you've recovered from your ordeal?"

Georgiana flushed slightly and nodded. A man,
somewhat older than Bella, had risen from the table
to watch them, an affectionate smile on his thin lips.

She felt forced to disclaim, "It was hardly an ordeal, ma'am."

"*Ma'am?* I thought I told you to call me Bella." Bella smiled mischievously. "And of course it was an ordeal. Fleeing from horrible Charles was always an ordeal."

Georgiana stopped and stared. "You know Charles?"

Bella's big blue eyes opened wide. "But of course. Didn't I mention it last night?"

When Georgiana shook her head, Bella tucked her arm in hers and drew her guest to the table.

"But we were neighbours; you know that. Of course, Charles came over to play sometimes. But he never got on with Dominic and the other boys, mainly because he was younger and always tried to show off. He used to tease me unmercifully. At least, he did if Dominic wasn't around. So, you see, I know just what it feels like to run away from your cousin Charles. And I can't think he's improved with age."

Standing by the chair beside her new friend, Georgiana shook her head. "I expect you're right." She looked expectantly at the man. He smiled and bowed slightly.

"Permit me to introduce myself, my dear. I'm afraid, if we wait for Bella to remember my existence, we might not be introduced until dinner."

"Oh, fustian!" said Bella, catching his hand and giving it a little shake. "My dear Georgiana, allow me to present my husband, Arthur."

Georgiana dropped a demure curtsy, hiding her surprise. She had not thought about Bella's husband at all, but would never have imagined the youthful Bella married to a man so much older. As she straightened, her eyes met his, grey and kindly, and she had the feeling of being read like a book. But then he smiled, such a sweet smile, and suddenly it no longer seemed so odd that Bella should be his wife.

"Miss Hartley. Might I say how pleased we are to welcome you to our home?"

Georgiana murmured her thanks.

Over breakfast, Lord Winsmere made little comment, but contented himself with listening as Bella and she discussed feminine interests.

"I see you are out of blacks," said Bella. "So fortunate."

Georgiana hesitated, then explained, "Actually, it's only four months since my father died, but he made me promise that I wouldn't go into mourning for him. But—" she shrugged slightly "—I thought greys and lilacs were a reasonable compromise."

Bella's candid gaze assessed her dispassionately. "I must say, if your father was a painter, I can understand why he was so insistent you stay out of black. With your skin, it would certainly not suit."

Georgiana grinned. "I'm not certain that wasn't at the back of his mind when he made his request."

As she turned her attention to her piece of toast, she was conscious of his lordship's grey eyes resting on her with approval.

In fact, Lord Winsmere was pleased to approve of his wife's prospective protégée. Georgiana Hartley, he decided, was a neat little thing. His eye had seen too many beauties to class her as one, but her features were pure and, with the gloss of a little animation, presently lacking, she could lay claim to the appellation of attractive with ease. She was petite, but her figure was full and delicately curved, not unlike Bella's curvaceous form. And, more important than any other quality, the girl from Italy was not missish. Which was just as well, if she was to deal with his forthright Bella. All in all, Bella's assessment had been accurate. Miss Georgiana Hartley was eminently acceptable.

When the ladies left him to his coffee and the morning's news-sheet, he spent some time in a blank study of the parlour door. Undoubtedly, Dominic had done right in sending Georgiana to Winsmere House. There was little hope such an attractive miss could find decent employment without subjecting herself to dangers he, for one, did not wish to contemplate. Dominic's plan to introduce her into society was a wise one. Thus far, the young lady seemed of a most amenable disposition. And, although not highly born, her lineage was not beneath consideration. He had checked for himself in the Register of Landowners. The Hartleys had been an unremarkable family for generations, but they were nevertheless of good stock. She would make some young squire an unexceptionable wife.

However, more importantly from his point of view, her presence would ease Bella's boredom. His darling had talked non-stop since rising this morning, a sure sign of happiness.

With a smile at his own susceptibilities, Lord Winsmere rose and, taking up his unread news-sheet, retired to the library. For once, Dominic seemed to have bestirred himself for purely philanthropic reasons. His scheme was in the girl's best interests and would keep Bella amused. There was no reason to interfere. Bella could entangle herself in the chit's life to her heart's content. Neither would take any ill. As his shrewd brain began to sort through the potential ramifications of his brother-in-law's plan, Lord Winsmere's brows rose. His lips curved slightly. In the end, who knew what might come of it?

"NOW, GEORGIE, promise me you won't put me to the blush," said Bella, firmly drawing on her gloves as the carriage drew to a standstill. "I couldn't endure it in front of Fancon. The woman's a terror. Lord only knows what damage she could do to your chances if she heard you asking about the price of a gown."

Georgiana blushed. The slight frown on her friend's face told her Bella was not yet convinced she had won their last battle. Georgiana simply couldn't see the necessity for new gowns for herself. Surely it was not a requirement for a companion to be fashionably dressed? But Bella had been adamant.

"Just wait until you *are* a companion before you start dressing like a dowd."

At Georgiana's instinctive and forlorn glance at her demure grey gown, Bella had been instantly contrite. "Oh, I don't mean that! Your gowns are perfectly acceptable, you know they are. It's just that for going out into society you need more...well, more society clothes. This is London, after all."

Finally, worn down by Bella's arguments, strengthened by the defection of Cruickshank, who had deciphered enough of their conversation to give her a hard stare, Georgiana had consented to accompany Bella to the salon of the modiste known as Fancon. It was her third day in London, and she was beginning to feel at home in the large mansion on Green Street. Lord Winsmere was all that was kind. And Bella, of course, was Bella. Georgiana was overwhelmed by their kindness. But not so overwhelmed that she would consent to Bella's buying her new gowns.

"If I must have new gowns to go about and become known, then of course I'll pay for them." Her calm statement had caused Bella to look at her in concern.

"But, my dear Georgie, gowns, you know...well, they're not all that... I mean to say..." The garrulous Bella had flustered to a halt.

The drift of her thoughts had reached Georgiana. "Oh! Did you think I have no money?"

Bella's eyes widened. "Well, I thought you might not be exactly flush, what with your trip and expecting your uncle to be there to help at the end of it."

Georgiana smiled affectionately. They had thought her a pauper but had still wanted to help. She knew enough of the world to appreciate such sentiments. "Not a bit of it. My father left me reasonably well to do—or at least, that's how my Italian solicitors described it. I don't know what exactly that means, but I have funds deposited here on which I may draw."

To her relief, Lord Winsmere had insisted on accompanying her to the bank her father had patronised. She had little doubt it was his lordship's standing that had resulted in such prompt and polite service. There had been no difficulty in establishing her *bona fides* through papers she had carried from Italy.

While waiting for the carriage to stop rocking, Georgiana glanced at Bella's profile. They had taken to each other as if each were the sister the other had never had. "Only two gowns, mind."

Bella turned, her eyes narrowing. "Two *day* gowns *and* an evening gown." She stared uncompromisingly at Georgiana.

With a wry grimace, Georgiana acquiesced. "All right. *And* an evening gown. But nothing too elaborate," she added, as the groom opened the door.

Together they entered the discreet establishment of Fancon. A woman dressed in severe black glided forward to greet them. Her black hair was pulled back and, it appeared to Georgiana, forcibly restrained in a tight bun. Black eyes, like gimlets, sharp and shuttered, assessed her. This, she soon learned, was the great Fancon herself. Imbued with suitable awe, Georgiana noted a certain restraint in the woman's manner and was careful to give no cause for offence.

Half an hour passed in the most pleasant of occupations. Fancon had numerous gowns to choose from. Georgiana tried on a great many. There were fabrics, too, which could be fashioned to any style she wished. Georgiana found Bella's interest infectious. And she could not resist the temptation to indulge in Fancon's elegant creations. However, true to her word, she chose only two day dresses, one in softest lilac, the other a deep mauve. Both suited her well, their high waists outlining her youthful figure. She feared that Fancon would be irritated by her meagre order, particularly after the woman had been so insistent she try on such a great number of gowns. Yet nothing but the most complete equanimity showed on the modiste's stern face.

Much discussion went into the creation of an evening gown. The styles which favoured her were easy enough to decide. Yet there was nothing suitable made up.

"Your colouring, Miss Hartley, is less pale than the norm. It is no matter. We will decide on the fabric, and I will have my seamstresses work up the gown by tomorrow." With a calm wave of her hand, Fancon summoned her underlings. They brought bolts of fine cloth, in mauves and lilacs. While Georgiana stood, wreathed in fabric, Bella and Fancon studied her critically. Georgiana, too, watched proceedings in the mirror.

"It must show you off to your greatest advantage," declared Bella.

Georgiana seriously doubted that companions were chosen for the picture they made in the ballroom.

Fancon turned and murmured a command. A minute later, a fresh selection of materials arrived. Sea-green gauze, spangled and shimmering, was draped around Georgiana. The assistant stood back, and Georgiana raised her eyes to the mirror. She gasped. Was the slim, slender mermaid she saw there really herself? The green brought out the lights in her hair and eyes, and emphasised the creaminess of her skin. She stood and stared. Then, slowly, she shook her head sadly.

"Not yet. I'm still in mourning, remember?"

Another murmur from Fancon saw a deep topaz silk

replace the sea-green gauze. Again, Georgiana stared. This time she looked almost as worldly as Bella. The silk added an air of allure, of mystery. She looked...enticing. But again she refused.

Apparently resigned to using the purplish hues, Fancon next produced a pale amethyst silk. Georgiana regarded it critically. The colour suited her well enough, making her appear soft and feminine. But the amethyst simply did not do for her what the previous two shades had. In this, she simply looked passably pretty. She turned and looked longingly at the topaz and the sea-green, lying discarded beside her. Still, she couldn't allow herself to be distracted from her purpose. Doubtless ladies who needed companions would approve of the amethyst silk.

"Yes. I'll take this fabric. And the pattern we agreed on."

Georgiana turned in time to catch the look that passed between Bella and Fancon. It was a look that bespoke an understanding, but she got no further clue to assist in its interpretation.

While they waited for the two day dresses to be packed, Georgiana reflected that Madame Fancon had not seemed anywhere near as dragon-like as Bella had led her to believe.

Settled in the barouche, with Fancon's boxes on the opposite seat, Bella leant forward and spoke to her coachman. "Once around the park for luck. Then back to Green Street."

The carriage moved off. Georgiana sat quietly, wondering a little at the revelations of the sumptuous sea-green and topaz silks. Could she really appear like that? Her? Little Georgiana?

Bella also sat quietly, smugly satisfied with the outcome of her scheming. She had been to see Fancon the day before, while Arthur had taken Georgiana to see her banker. The modiste knew her well; she was, after all, one of her best customers. Fancon had been most helpful, particularly after she had let fall the information that a certain peer was most desirous that Georgiana should be well presented, and hence money was no option. Dominic could hardly take exception to that. Bella grinned. She had little doubt Fancon would guess who the gentleman was. Who other than her brother would be likely to leave a young girl in her care?

"Bella, there's been some mistake. We have six boxes instead of two."

Georgiana's words reclaimed Bella's attention. She turned and found Georgiana frowning at the offending extra boxes. "No, no," said Bella. "It's all right. I bought some gowns, too. I couldn't resist after seeing you in them, and we're much of a size." All of which, Bella told her conscience, was perfectly true.

Georgiana raised her brows but said no more.

Bella returned to her absent-minded contemplation of the pavements. Undoubtedly she'd have to argue hard and fast to get Georgiana to accept the gowns she had bought. But none of them were in colours she, so much darker of hair and fairer of skin, could wear. The sea-green gauze and topaz silk would look hideous on her. They were to be delivered tomorrow, along with the amethyst silk. Surely Georgie would see what a waste it would be simply to throw them away?

As the barouche turned into the park, Bella sat up straighter. She looked across at Georgiana, sitting quietly beside her. Demure she might look, but Georgiana Hartley had a mind of her own. Stubborn to a fault, she was sure to balk at accepting what she would probably class as charity. Still, Bella was perfectly certain Dominic would have wanted her to spend his money as she had. She was sure he would approve, when he saw Georgiana in the topaz silk. And, after all, Georgiana should be grateful enough to want to please her brother. She made a mental note to remember Dominic, if she had need of further ammunition to force Georgiana to accept the gowns.

"IT'S MY 'at home' this afternoon." Bella came bustling into the downstairs parlour.

Georgiana looked up from the magazine she was idly leafing through. She felt supremely confident this morning, arrayed in one of her new gowns, a soft bluey lilac cambric. Bella's elegance seemed less daunting now. She caught Bella's eye as it rested pensively upon her. Georgiana raised one fine brow in invitation.

"About the story we should tell about you. To account for your being here."

"What about the truth?" asked Georgiana, not quite sure what her friend meant.

"Well, yes. The truth, of course. But…do you think the whole truth's wise?"

When Georgiana looked her confusion, Bella continued, "You see, if you tell about how you met Dominic, people might get the wrong idea. To support your story, you'd have to explain about Charles. And, my dear, if you're looking for a position, the last person you would want to claim kinship with is Charles."

Bella had put a great deal of thought into how best to broach this most delicate of subjects. Now she watched Georgiana carefully to see how the younger girl took her suggestion. Georgiana was frowning, her thoughts clouding her big eyes.

"You mean…?"

"What I mean," said Bella, candid to a fault, "is that Charles is hardly a gold-plated reference. But there's really no need to mention him at all. All we have to do is decide how you came to stay with me. I think the most sensible thing to say is that we had met, years ago, at Candlewick, before you went to Italy. We became such friends that we've been corresponding ever since. Naturally, when you returned to England and found your uncle dead, you came back to London to stay with me. That should be believable enough, don't you think?" When Georgiana made no reply, Bella pressed her final argument. "And you wouldn't want to put Dominic in a difficult position, would you?"

Put Lord Alton in a difficult position? For a minute, Georgiana could make no sense of her friend's allusion. Then the Fragonard materialised in her mind's eye…and the image of his lordship as she had last seen him, a vision that had not yet faded from her memory.

"Oh."

Of course. Georgiana gave herself a mental shake. She wasn't so innocent that she couldn't follow Bella's drift. While her visit with Lord Alton had been utterly without consequence, society, if it heard of it, might view it otherwise. She raised her gaze to Bella's face. "I'll do whatever you think best. I wouldn't want to cause your brother any trouble."

Bella grinned, entirely satisfied.

"Oh, and one last thing. It will be better, at this stage, if we make no mention of your wish for a position. Such things are better negotiated after you're known."

Georgiana nodded her acceptance, Lord Alton's assurance that his sister knew what was best echoing in her mind.

That afternoon three matrons came to tea, bringing with them a gaggle of unmarried daughters. Georgiana did not succeed in fixing which young ladies belonged to which mama. In the end, it made little difference. To a woman, they accepted Bella's charmingly phrased explanation of her presence. Quick eyes surveyed the latest entrant in the marriage game. The ladies found no reason not to be gracious. Miss Hartley was no beauty.

Miss Hartley had difficulty subduing her mirth. They were really so blatant in their pursuit of well heeled and preferably titled son-in-laws.

To her surprise, Georgiana found conversing with the younger ladies almost beyond her. Used to dealing with the gracious conversation of the Italian aristocracy, among whom she had spent much of her life, used to the subtle ebb and flow of polished discourse, she found it hard to relate to the titters and smirks and girlish giggles of the four very proper English maids. However, she did not make the mistake of attempting to join the matrons. Stoically, she bore her ordeal as best she could.

Bella, watching her, was pleased by her confidence and innate poise. Innocent and trusting Georgiana might be, but she was no mindless ninny, scared to open her mouth in company. Her manners were assured, unusually so for a girl of her age.

When the guests had departed, Bella grimaced at Georgiana. "Witless, aren't they?" She smiled at Georgiana's emphatic nod. "They're not all like that, of course. Still, there are a lot of unbelievably silly girls about." Bella paused, considering her words. "Just as well, I suppose. There are an awful lot of silly men, too."

They shared a grin of complete understanding.

Five minutes later, just as they had settled comfortably to their embroidery, Johnson entered. "Lady Winterspoon, m'lady."

Bella rose. Georgiana was disconcerted to see perturbation in her friend's blue eyes. Then Lady Winterspoon was in the room.

"Bella! Haven't seen you in ages! Where've you been hiding yourself?"

Lady Winterspoon's trenchant accents reverberated through the room. Bella suffered a hug and a hearty kiss and, looking slightly shaken, settled her ageing guest in an armchair. Lady Winterspoon was, Georgiana guessed, quite old enough to be Bella's mother. Who was she?

"Amelia, I'd like you to meet Georgiana Hartley. She's an old friend of mine from the country. Georgiana, this is my sister-in-law."

Georgiana met the clear grey gaze and found herself smiling warmly in response. Lord Winsmere's sister, of course.

"Hartley, hmm? Well, I probably knew your father, if he's the one I'm thinking of. Painter fellow. Jimmy? James? Married Lorien Putledge."

Georgiana nodded, eager to hear more of her parents. She had never before met anyone who had known them in their younger days.

Reading her interest in her eyes, Lady Winterspoon waved one hand in a negative gesture. "No, my dear. I can't tell you much about them; I didn't know them that well. I take it they've passed on?"

Disappointed, Georgiana nodded. Bella promptly stepped in with their agreed explanation for her presence in Green Street. Lady Winterspoon's shrewd eyes remained on Georgiana throughout Bella's speech. Whether she accepted the story, neither young woman felt qualified to say.

"Hmph!" was all the response she made.

After a moment of silence, during which both Bella and Georgiana racked their brains to think of something to say, Lady Winterspoon commented, "Dare say you'll make quite a hit. Not just in the common way. In the circumstances, not a bad thing to be."

Georgiana decided that was meant as a compliment. She smiled.

Lady Winterspoon's lips twitched. She turned purposefully to Bella. "But that's not why I came. Bella, you've got to have a word with that brother of yours. Elaine Changley's becoming entirely too much, with her airs and graces and subtle suggestions she'll be the next Viscountess Alton.'' Lady Winterspoon snorted.

Bella frowned and bit her lip. She cast a slightly scandalised look Georgiana's way. But Georgiana was too engrossed in Lady Winterspoon's disclosures to notice.

''If I thought there was any chance of it coming to pass, I'd insist Arthur break the connection. Elaine Changley! Why, she's...'' Amelia Winterspoon became aware of Georgiana's clear hazel gaze. She broke off. ''Well, you know what I mean,'' she amended, glaring at Bella.

Relieved at the opportune halt to her sister-in-law's tirade, Bella gracefully seated herself on the sofa. ''Amelia, you know I have no influence whatever with Dominic.''

''Pshaw! You'd have influence enough if you chose to use it!''

Bella coloured slightly. ''I assure you I share your concern about Lady Changley, but mentioning her to Dominic is entirely beyond me.''

''Well, Elaine Changley is beyond the pale! Just bear that in mind. You'll look no-how if you wake up one morning to find her your sister-in-law.''

Lady Winterspoon heaved herself up. ''Must go. Just wanted to let you know things need a bit of push from you.'' She fixed her grey gaze firmly on Bella.

Despite her annoyance, Bella could not help grinning back. She rose.

Lady Winterspoon paused to nod to Georgiana.

"I'll see you at Almack's, my dear." She turned to Bella. "I'll get Emily to send you vouchers."

"Thank you," said Bella, taken aback. She had forgotten Amelia had the ear of several of the patronesses of Almack's. She went out with Lady Winterspoon.

Minutes later, returning to the back parlour, Bella found Georgiana staring into space. She shut the door with a click, jolting her guest to attention. "Well!" she said, with determined brightness. "Vouchers for Almack's without even having to charm one of the patronesses. We'll go just as soon as Lady Cowper sends them."

"Yes, of course," said Georgiana. But it was plain to Bella that her friend was absorbed in distant thoughts...thoughts she made no move to share.

CHAPTER THREE

BELLA HEARD the door of her boudoir open and shut, but, absorbed in brushing the haresfoot delicately over her cheekbones, she did not turn around. In her mirror, she saw Hills obediently drop a curtsy and leave. Finally, satisfied with her appearance, she swung about. "Arthur— Oh! Dominic!"

She was out of her chair and across the room on the word.

Half laughing, half frowning, Dominic held her off. "No! Compose yourself, you hoyden. What will staid Arthur think? And I can't have you ruining my cravat as you did the last time."

So Bella had to make do with clasping his hands. "Oh, thank you, dearest Dominic, for sending Georgie to me! We're having such a wonderful time!" She drew him down to plant a sisterly kiss on one lean cheek.

Dominic suffered the embrace, using the moment to cast a knowledgeable eye over his sister. "So you and Miss Hartley have hit it off?"

"Famously!" Bella sat with a swirl of her satin skirts. "But whoever would have thought you'd...?" She broke off, biting her lip.

Dominic's black brows rose. There was a disconcerting glint in his eye, but his voice was gentle when he softly prompted, "I'd...?"

Bella flushed and turned back to her dressing-table, skirts rustling, and busied herself with a pot of rouge. She refused to meet his eye. "That you'd behave so uncommonly sensible, if you must know. From everything I've heard, it must be the first time in weeks!"

"Weeks?" The arrogant black brows rose again. Dominic considered the point for all of ten seconds. "Feels more like years."

Bella, surprised by his weary tone, chanced a glance at him in the mirror. He raised his head at that moment, and she was caught in his chilly blue gaze. "That aside, dear sister mine, you would be well advised not to listen to gossip—about myself, or anyone else, for that matter."

Eyes wide, Bella knew better than to remonstrate. Dominic was ten years her senior and had been the strictest of guardians in the years preceding her marriage. She half expected some more pointed rebuke, but he turned aside, a far-away look settling over his handsome face. To her, that pensive look was far more frightening than Amelia's bluster. Surely he wasn't serious about Elaine Changley?

She waited, but he made no further remark. Finally she asked, "Will you stay for dinner?"

He looked up.

Bella fidgeted with her hairbrush. "Georgie and I are going on to Almack's later, so you needn't fear you'll have to kick your heels in my drawing-room."

Her tone brought a smile to her brother's face, dispelling the withdrawn look which had so concerned her. Still, she was sure he would refuse.

Instead, after a moment's hesitation, she heard him murmur, "Why not?"

As it seemed a purely rhetorical question, Bella made no attempt to answer it.

Dominic shrugged, then turned his sweetest smile full on her. "Since you ask, dear sister, I'll stay. It might be interesting to meet my...*your* protégée."

As Bella reached for the bell-pull to summon Hills, Dominic surveyed a nearby chair through his quizzing-glass. Reassured, he carefully disposed his long limbs in the delicate piece.

"So how came you to get vouchers for the Marriage Mart so soon?"

"Well! It was the most fortunate thing!" Bella seized on the question to lead the conversation on to lighter ground, hoping her intrusion into her brother's private life would be the quicker forgotten. Dominic had never allowed her any speculation on the possible candidates for the position of Viscountess Alton. And she had long ago learned that any mention of his mistresses, past, present or potential, was sure to invite one of his more painful set-downs. Still, after Amelia's warning, and her own unfortunate gaffe, she had felt justified in at least trying to broach the subject.

While Hills informed Johnson of the necessity of setting an extra place and returned to twist her hair into an elegant knot, Bella described the recent history of Georgiana Hartley. As she prattled, she watched her brother's face in the mirror. He sat quietly studying his nails, paying scant attention to her words. His lack

of interest worried her. She had hardly expected him
to be seriously concerned with Georgiana. After all,
he had barely met her and she was certainly not the
sort of woman to hold his attention. But his introspec-
tion was unusual and disquieting, suggesting as it did
the existence of some weightier matter dragging on
his mind. Like matrimony. But surely, *surely,* he
wouldn't choose Elaine Changley?

It was with relief that Bella finally rose from her
dressing-table. What with the distraction of Dominic's
arrival, the hour was well advanced. He accompanied
her down the wide staircase and entered the drawing-
room by her side.

Georgiana was talking to Arthur. Warned by his
face that someone unexpected had entered, she turned
and was trapped, once again without warning, in the
blue of Lord Alton's eyes.

The same eyes that haunted her dreams.

For Georgiana, it was a definite case of *déjà vu.* Her
breathing stopped; her heart contracted. Her gaze was
oddly restricted, the rest of the room fading away,
leaving one strong face to impress itself on her mind.
Her stare widened to take in his immaculate evening
clothes, and the way his dark hair sat in elegant waves
about his head. A cornflower-blue sapphire winked in
his cravat, its colour no more intense than his eyes.

Then, thankfully, Arthur moved forward to greet his
guest.

The worst was past. Georgiana's natural poise reas-
serted itself and she could function again. Then Lord
Alton turned to take her hand. His clasp was cool and
gentle. He smiled and bowed elegantly.

"Miss Hartley. So we meet again. I do hope Bella hasn't been tiring you out with her gadding."

To Georgiana's intense chagrin, her tongue promptly tied itself in knots and her voice deserted her. She managed to force out a weak, "Of course not, my lord," around the constriction in her throat. What on earth was the matter with her?

Luckily, Johnson entered to announce dinner. Inwardly, Georgiana heaved a sigh of relief. But relief died a sudden death when she discovered Lord Alton was dining at his sister's board. Naturally, he sat opposite her. Throughout the meal, which could have been the meanest fare for all she noticed, Georgiana struggled to avoid looking directly at the gentleman opposite, with mixed success. Arthur unwittingly came to her rescue, turning the conversation into political waters. He engaged his brother-in-law in a detailed discussion of the Corn Laws, leaving the ladies to their own interests.

As Bella seemed abstracted, Georgiana confined her gaze, if not her attention, to her plate. As course followed course, and the gentlemen's discourse continued unabated, she was conscious of a growing irritation. Admittedly her awkwardness in the drawing-room had hardly been encouraging, but Lord Alton could at least make the effort to address some remark to her. Perhaps, in England, it was not done to talk across the table, even at family meals.

When the sweets appeared before her, Bella shook herself and glanced about. Only then did she notice that her husband and brother had embarked on a most tedious discussion, leaving poor Georgie to herself. It was on the tip of her tongue to call attention to their lapse of manners, when she recalled that neither gentleman would feel the least inhibited about alluding to her own brown study of the past hour, nor in asking the subject of said study. As she had no intention of once again drawing her brother's fire, she turned instead to Georgiana.

"You see what it is to dine *en famille* in Winsmere House? Pearls before swine, my dear. Here we sit, only too willing to be enthralled, and all they can think of is their political problems." Her eyes twinkled at her husband, sitting opposite her at the head of the table.

Unperturbed by her attack, he smiled back. "In truth, I'm surprised to see you still here. I had thought you were off to Almack's tonight."

Bella's eyes swung to the clock, peacefully ticking away on the sideboard. "Heavens! I'd no idea. Georgie, we'll have to bustle. Come. We'll leave our two fine gentlemen to their port."

Both men stood as she rose.

Georgiana perforce rose too. She could not resist throwing one last glance at the tall figure opposite her. To her confusion, she found he was watching her. But his face bore nothing more than a remotely polite expression. He returned her nod with genial but distant civility.

As the ladies departed the room, Arthur turned to his brother-in-law. "If you have the time, I'd value your opinions on how best to go about this business."

Dominic started slightly, as if his mind had wandered from the matter they had been discussing for the past hour. "Yes. Of course." His usual, sleepily bored smile appeared. "I'd be only too delighted, naturally."

Arthur, not deceived, laughed. "Which means you'd much rather be elsewhere, discussing more enthralling subjects, but you will, of course, humour your host. You, Dominic, are a complete hand. Why you must belittle your efforts in this I know not."

By unspoken agreement, they moved to the door. Dominic waved one languid hand, and a priceless sapphire caught the light. "Perhaps because my—er—efforts, as you term them, are so undemanding as to be positively valueless."

Arthur was surprised into a snort. "Valueless? Who else, pray tell, has succeeded in even introducing the subject in Prinny's presence?"

They entered the library and made for the two large armchairs by the hearth.

"Introducing the subject's hardly the same as gaining His Highness's support." Dominic sank into one chair, stretching his long legs before him and emitting a weary sigh.

Arthur glanced sharply at him. "You know that's not necessary. Just as long as His Highness is aware of how things stand. That'll be more than enough." He handed Dominic a cut-crystal glass filled with his oldest port, then settled comfortably in the chair opposite.

Silence fell, broken only by the ticking of the long case clock in the corner and a sudden crackle as a log settled in the grate. Arthur, who had had plenty of opportunity to observe his brother-in-law over dinner, and to note the arrested expression in those startlingly blue eyes whenever they rested on Georgiana Hartley, continued to watch the younger man, waiting patiently for whatever came next, confident that something, indeed, would be forthcoming.

Finally, Dominic's gaze sought his face. "This Miss Hartley I've foisted on you... I assume you approve?"

Arthur nodded. "Georgiana is exactly the sort of company Bella needs. You have my heartfelt thanks for sending her to us."

The black brows rose. "Seemed the least I could do." Dominic's face showed evidence of distraction, as it frequently had that night. Arthur's lips twitched. He sternly repressed the impulse to smile.

Eventually Dominic shook off his abstraction sufficiently to comment, "Bella was saying she's becoming rather stubbornly taken with this idea of hiring out as a companion. She seemed to think that she, Miss Hartley, might take things into her own hands. That, I need hardly say, will simply not do."

Arthur nodded gravely. "I entirely agree. Also, I have to concur with Bella on her reading of Georgiana's character." He paused to steeple his fingers, and stared into the fire over the top of the structure. "Georgiana is clearly unused to relying on the bounty of others. It irks her, I think, to be living, as it were, on our charity. She has some money of her own, but not, I suspect, the requisite fortune. She has spoken to me about the best way to go about hiring herself out. I returned an evasive and, I hope, restraining answer. Luckily, the fact that she has been out of England for so long makes it relatively easy to make excuses which on the face of it are reasonable, without going into over-many details. However—'' he smiled at Dominic ''—beneath that demure exterior lies a great deal of strength and not a little courage. From what I gather, she made her way to England virtually unaided—not an inconsiderable feat. I seriously doubt she'll accept our vague answers for much longer.''

A black frown of quite dramatic proportions dominated the Viscount's face.

Arthur suppressed a grin. Finally he asked, ''Do you have any ideas?''

Still frowning, Dominic slowly shook his head. Then he glanced at Arthur. ''Do you?''

''As a matter of fact, I do.'' Arthur straightened his shoulders and prepared to explain. His grey gaze rested thoughtfully on Dominic's face. ''Bella, of course, needs distraction. Essentially, that means a companion. But can you imagine how she would feel if I insisted she hire one?''

Dominic's frown lightened.

''Bella has been most assiduous in helping Georgiana and, from what I've seen, Georgiana is truly grateful. I plan to suggest to Georgiana, in confidence, that she become Bella's companion in truth. However, in order to spare Bella's quite natural feelings, the arrangement will be a secret between the two of us. To all outward appearances, which of course must include the servants, she will continue as a guest in this house.'' Arthur's brows rose interrogatively. ''Do you think that'll pass?''

Dominic grinned. ''I'm sure it will. How useful to be able to turn your talents to something other than politics.'' His grin broadened into a smile. ''And no wonder you're so invaluable in your present capacity.''

Arthur smiled and inclined his head. "As you say." For a moment he regarded the younger man intently. Then, almost imperceptibly, he shrugged. "I'll speak to Georgiana in the morning. It would be wise, I suspect, to ensure she has no opportunity to take the bit between her teeth.''

"Thank you, my lord." Georgiana curtsied and watched young Lord Mortlake mince away across the floor. Still, at least he had danced well.

She flicked open her fan and plied it ruthlessly. The large, sparsely furnished rooms which were Almack's were crammed with bodies dressed in silks and satins of every conceivable hue. The day had been unseasonably warm, and the evening, initially balmy, had turned sultry. The air in the rooms hung oppressively. Ostrich feathers wilted. As a particularly limp pair, dyed puce, bobbed by, attached to the head-dress of an extremely conscious beauty, Georgiana hid her smirk behind her fan.

Her eyes scanned the company. Other than Bella, standing by her side, engaged in a low-voiced conversation with an elderly matron, Georgiana knew only those few people Bella had thus far introduced her to. And, she reflected, none of them needed a companion.

As her eyes feasted on the spectrum of colours mingling before her, she spared a smile for her sartorial elegance. By comparison with many about her, she was underdressed. The pattern of Fancon's amethyst silk robe was simple and plain, with long, clean lines uncluttered by frills and furbelows. Her single strand of pearls, inherited from her mother, shone warmly about her neck. Originally uncertain, she now felt smugly satisfied with her appearance.

Thoughts of dresses brought her earlier discovery to mind, together with the subsequent argument with Bella. How on earth could she accept the sea-green gauze and topaz silk dresses from Bella, to whom she was already so deeply indebted? Yet it was undeniable that Bella could not wear them. Both dresses were presently hanging in the wardrobe in her chamber. She had been quite unable to persuade Bella to repack and return them. What was she to do about them?

The idea that, if she had been wearing the topaz silk gown that evening, Lord Alton would have paid more attention to her flitted through her mind. Ruthlessly, she stamped on the errant thought. She was here to find employment, not ogle lords. And what possible interest could Lord Alton have in her—an unremarkable country lass, not even at home in England?

Depressed, by that thought and the lowering fact she had not yet made any headway in finding a position, Georgiana determinedly looked over the sea of heads, pausing on the occasional powdered wig that belonged to a previous generation. Maybe, beneath one, she would find someone to hire her?

"Here, girl! Georgiana, ain't it? Come and help me to that chair."

Georgiana whirled to find Lady Winterspoon beside her. The old lady was leaning on a cane.

Seeing her glancé, Amelia Winterspoon chuckled. "I only use it at night. Helps me get the best seats."

Georgiana smiled and obediently took her ladyship's arm. Once settled in a gilt chair by the wall, Lady Winterspoon waved Georgiana to its partner beside her.

"I can only take so much of this place. Too much mindless talk addles the brain."

Georgiana felt the sharp grey eyes assessing her. She wondered whether she would pass muster.

A wry smile twisted Amelia Winterspoon's thin lips. "Just as I thought. *Not* in the common style."

The old lady paused. Georgiana had the impression she was reliving long-ago evenings spent under the candlelight of ballroom chandeliers. Then, abruptly, the grey gaze sharpened and swung to her face.

"If you're old enough to heed advice, here's one piece you should take to heart. You ain't a beauty, but you're no antidote either. You're different—and not just because you're fair when the current craze is for dark. The most successful women who've ever trod these boards were those who were brave enough to be themselves."

"Themselves?"

"Themselves," came the forceful answer. "Don't put on airs, nor pretend to be what you ain't. Thankfully, you seem in no danger of doing that. Don't try to ape the English misses. Don't try to lose your foreignness—use it instead. All you need to make a go of it is to smile and enjoy yourself. The rest'll come easy."

"But—" Georgiana wondered whether she should

explain her situation to Arthur's sister. Maybe she could help her find a position?

"No buts, girl! Just do it! There's no point in wasting your life away being a wallflower. Get out and enjoy yourself." Lady Winterspoon used her cane to gesture at the dance-floor. "Now go on—off you go!"

Despite the conviction that she should feel piqued at such forthright meddling, Georgiana found herself grinning, then laughing as Lady Winterspoon nodded encouragingly. Rising, Georgiana swept a curtsy to her ladyship, now comfortably ensconced, and, a smile lingering on her lips, returned to the throng. She made her way to where she had left Bella.

But Bella was no longer in sight.

Perturbed, Georgiana stood still and wondered what to do. She could go back and sit with Lady Winterspoon, only she would probably drive her off again. English social strictures were not Georgiana's strong suit. Still, she rather suspected she should not wander about the rooms alone. Suddenly she realised she was frowning.

Lady Winterspoon's strong voice still echoed in her mind. "Enjoy yourself!"

Georgiana lifted her head. She had been introduced to Italian society at the age of sixteen. Surely, at the ripe old age of eighteen, she could manage such a simple social occasion as this? Consciously drawing about herself the cloak of social calm her father's female patrons had impressed on her was the hallmark of a lady, she stepped out more confidently to search for Bella—not hurriedly, in a frenzy, but in a calm and dignified way, smiling as she went.

As she moved slowly down the room, truly looking about her for the first time that evening, she heard snatches of conversation wafting from the groups she passed.

"Did you see that Emma Michinford? Making such sheep's eyes at…"

"Well, we all know what *he's* after!"

"She's really rather pathetic, don't you agree?"

"Not that it'll come to anything, mark my words. The likes of him…"

Waspish, biting, cutting gibes… The comments blurred into a melody typical, Georgiana suspected, of the place. Her smile grew.

"Oh!" Her elbow jogged that of another stroller. "I'm so sorry. Pray excuse me."

"Gladly, my dear, if you'll tell me what could possibly be so amusing in Almack's."

The languid tones of the gentleman bowing before her were, Georgiana judged, devoid of menace. He was very neatly and correctly attired, soberly so. His blue coat was well cut, his satin breeches without a crease. Brown hair, stylishly but not rakishly cut, framed a pleasant face. There was nothing one could put a finger on to account for the air of elegance which clung to him.

As he continued to look at her with mild curiosity, Georgiana, Lady Winterspoon's dictum still fresh in her mind, answered him truthfully. "It was merely the conversation, caught in snippets as I walked about. It's—" she put her head on one side as she considered her words "—rather single-minded, if you know what I mean."

A quirky grin twisted the gentleman's lips. "I do indeed know what you mean, Miss...?"

Having embarked on her course, Georgiana dispensed with caution, "Hartley. Georgiana Hartley. I'm staying with Lady Winsmere. I seem to have lost her in the crush."

"Ah, the lovely Bella. I think I saw her over by the door, in earnest conversation with Lady Duckworth. Permit me to escort you to her."

With only a single blink, Georgiana laid her gloved hand on the proffered sleeve. If she was going to be escorted by any gentleman tonight, she was quite content that it should be this one. He hadn't told her his name, but he seemed thoroughly at home.

"From your comment, you seem almost to laugh at the purpose of this great institution. Yet surely you propose to avail yourself of its services?"

This was the sort of conversation Georgiana had cut her social eye-teeth on. "I most certainly intend to avail myself of its services, but not, I think, as you might assume."

Her companion digested this riposte, before countering, "If that means you are not here to snare a title, or a fortune, what possible other use for this place can you have found?"

"Why, that to which I was putting it when you met me."

A pause developed, followed by a great sigh. "Very well. I confess myself stumped. What is it you've discovered within these faded grey walls?"

Georgiana smiled, eyes dancing. "Why, enjoyment, of course. I was enjoying myself." To her surprise, she realised this was true. She turned to glance into her companion's grey eyes. In them, she saw thunder-struck amazement.

"*Enjoyment?* In Almack's?"

Georgiana laughed. "Of course. I'm enjoying my-self now. Aren't you?"

Her gentleman stopped stock-still, a ludicrous mix-ture of horror and humour in his face. "Dreadful! I'll never live this down." Then his face cleared and he smiled, quite genuinely, at Georgiana. "Come, Miss Hartley. Let me restore you to Lady Winsmere. You're clearly too potent a force to be let loose for long."

Perfectly content, Georgiana strolled by his side through the crowd, who, she now noticed, seemed to part before them. Even before she caught sight of Bella's surprised face, she had started to question the identity of her escort. But she was determined not to worry. And, thankfully, whoever he was, her escort seemed to find nothing amiss.

Bella curtsied and chatted animatedly, but Georgi-ana still heard no name. With a final, *sotto voce,* "En-joying oneself in Almack's. Whatever next?" the very correct gentleman withdrew.

Georgiana turned to Bella, but, before she could ut-ter her question, Bella was exclaiming, albeit in de-lighted whispers, "Georgie! However did you do it?"

"Do what? Who is he?" Instinctively, Georgiana whispered too.

"Who? But...don't you know?" Bella stared in dis-belief, first at her, then at the elegant retreating back.

"No. No one introduced us. I bumped into him and apologised."

Bella fanned herself frantically. "Heavens! He might have cut you!"

"Cut...? But who on earth is he?"

"Brummel! George Brummel. He's one of society's most powerful arbiters of taste." Bella turned to survey Georgiana appraisingly. "Well! Obviously he's taken to you. What a relief! I didn't know what to think when I saw you with him. He can be quite diabolical, you know."

Georgiana, conscious now of the envious eyes upon her, smiled confidently. "You needn't have worried. We were just enjoying ourselves."

Bella looked incredulous.

Georgiana laughed.

"GOODNIGHT, Johnson."

"Goodnight, my lord."

The door of Winsmere House shut softly behind Dominic. The night continued mild, but the low rumble of distant thunder heralded the end of the unseasonal warmth. Still, Alton House in Grosvenor Square was only five minutes away. Dominic set off, swinging his slim ebony cane, his long strides unhurried as he headed for North Audley Street.

The evening had left him with a sense of dissatisfaction which he was hard put to explain. He had broken his journey to Brighton to check on Miss Hartley, although, to be precise, it was more to relieve his mind over whether Arthur and Bella had been put out over her descent on them. Thankfully, all had turned out for the best. Arthur's scheme would undoubtedly pave the way for Georgiana Hartley to spend the upcoming

Little Season with Bella, after which it would be wonderful if she had not received at least one acceptable proposal. The girl was not a brilliant match, but a perfectly suitable connection for any of the lesser nobility who made up the bulk of the *ton*. He had checked on her antecedents and knew them to be above reproach. Yes, Georgiana Hartley would very likely soon be betrothed. Which was far more appropriate than being a companion.

As he swung south into North Audley Street, Dominic grinned. How typical of Arthur to concoct such a perfect solution to the girl's troubles. And Bella's. Everything seemed set to fall smoothly into place. Which, all things considered, should leave him feeling smugly satisfied. Instead, he was feeling uncommonly irritated. The grin faded. A frown settled over his features.

A watchman passed by unobtrusively, unwilling to draw the attention of such a well set up and clearly out-of-sorts gentleman to his activities. Dominic heard him but gave no sign.

Why should he be feeling so disillusioned, so disheartened? He'd been living this life for the past twelve years. Why had it suddenly palled? The circumstances that had driven him to seek the peace of Candlewick drifted into his mind. All the glamour and glitter and laughter associated with the doings of the Carlton House set. And the underlying vice, the predictability, the sheer falsity of most of it—these were what had sent him scurrying for sanctuary. But even Candlewick had failed to lift his mood. While its serenity had been comforting, the huge house had seemed lonely, empty. He had never noticed it before; now its silence was oppressive.

The corner of Grosvenor Square loomed ahead. Dominic swung left and crossed the road to the railed garden. The gates were locked at sunset, but that had never stopped him strolling the well tended lawns by night. He vaulted the wrought-iron railings with accustomed ease, then turned his steps across the lawns in the direction of his town house on the south side of the Square. Tucking his cane under his arm, he thrust his hands into his coat pockets and sank his chin into the soft folds of his cravat. Doubtless, if he were still in the care of his old nurse, she would tell him to take one of Dr James's Powders. The blue devils, that was what he had.

A vision of honey-gold eyes crystallised in his brain. Why on earth Georgiana Hartley's eyes, together with the rest of her, should so plague him he could not understand. He was not a callow youth, to be so besotted with a female's finer points. He had hardly exchanged two words with the chit, yet, throughout the evening, had been aware of her every movement, every inflexion, every expression.

Leaves from the beech trees had piled in drifts and softly scrunched underfoot. Dominic paused to regard his feet, lightly covered with golden leaves. Then he shook his head, trying to rid it of the memory of curls sheening guinea-gold under candlelight. God! What was this? The onset of senility?

Determined to force his mind to sanity, he removed his hands from his pockets and straightened his shoulders. Ten long strides brought him to the fence, and he vaulted over to the pavement beyond. A few days, not to mention nights, of Elaine Changley's company would cure him of this idiotic fancy. As his feet crossed the cobbles, he commanded his memory to supply a vision of Lady Changley as he had last seen her, reclining amid the much rumpled sheets of the bed he had just vacated. Of course, Elaine's ambitions were on a par with her charms. But as he was as well acquainted with the former as he was with the latter he felt justified in ignoring them. A smile played at the corners of his fine lips as he trod the steps to his front door.

In the instant he raised his cane to beat a tattoo on the solid oak door, an unnerving vision in which Georgiana Hartley was substituted for Elaine Changley flooded his brain. So breathtaking was the sight that Dominic froze. The gold top of his cane, yet to touch the door, remained suspended before him.

The door opened and Dominic found himself facing his butler, Timms.

"My lord?"

Feeling decidedly foolish, Dominic lowered his cane. He sauntered past Timms, one of Duckett's protégés, as if it were perfectly normal for him to stand rooted to his own doorstep. He paused in the hallway to draw off his gloves, then handed the offending cane to Timms.

"I'll be leaving for Brighton early tomorrow, Timms. Tell Maitland to be ready about nine."

"Very good, m'lord."

Frowning, Dominic slowly ascended the gently curving staircase, pausing, as was his habit, to check his fob watch against the long case clock on the landing. Restoring his watch to his pocket, he reflected that, if nothing else could cure him of his disturbing affliction, the decadent amusements to be found within the Prince Regent's pavilion at Brighton would.

BY THE TIME the Winsmere House ladies were handed into their coach for the drive home from King Street, Georgiana had had proved to her, over and over again, the truth of Lady Winterspoon's dictum. If she enjoyed herself, then her partners seemed to enjoy her company. If she laughed, then they laughed, too. And, while such overt behaviour did not sit well with one brought up to the self-effacing manners expected of young Italian girls, it was a great deal better, to Georgiana's way of thinking, than simpering and giggling. Her upbringing clearly had not conditioned her for English social life. Nevertheless, the unrufflable calm she had been instructed was a lady's greatest asset certainly helped, allowing her to cloak her instinctive responses to some of those she had met—like Lord Ormskirk and his leering glances, and Mr Morecombe, with his penchant for touching her bare arms.

"The Sotherbys are holding a ball next week. Lady Margaret said she'd send cards." Bella's voice came out of the gloom of the seat opposite. "After tonight, I've no doubts we'll be kept busy. So fortunate, your meeting with Brummel."

The unmistakable sound of a smothered yawn came to Georgiana's ears. She smiled into the darkness. Despite her tiredness, Bella seemed even more excited by her success than she was. She had originally found her hostess's claim of boredom difficult to believe. Now she could find it in her to understand that, without any special interest, the balls and parties could indeed turn flat. Still, to her, everything was too new for there to be any danger of her own interest flagging before Bella's did. Hopefully Bella would not feel too let down when she found a position and moved away. Into obscurity. Georgiana frowned.

If she had been asked, five days previously, whether she had any ambition to enter the *ton,* she would unhesitatingly have disclaimed all such desire. However, having now had a small sample of the diverse entertainments to be found amid the social whirl, she rather thought she might enjoy being able to savour these, in moderation, by way of a change from the quieter lifestyle she considered her milieu. A saying of her father's drifted past her mind's ear. "Experience, girl! There's nothing quite like it and no substitute known.'

As the clop of the horses' hoofs echoed back from the tiered façades of the houses they passed, Georgiana puzzled over her change of heart. Still, nothing could alter the fact that she would need to earn her way, at least to some extent. That being so, perhaps she should take this opportunity of experiencing the *ton,* of enjoying herself amid the glittering throng? According to Bella, she needed to be known to find a position. So, until she secured one, she could, and perhaps should, follow her father's and Lady Winterspoon's advice.

Bella yawned. "Oh, dear. I'd forgotten what it was like." Another yawn was stifled behind one slim white-gloved hand. Then, "I wonder if Dominic has managed to convince Charles to sell the Place yet?"

The question jolted Georgiana out of her reverie. "Lord Alton wishes to buy the Place?"

"Why, yes. Didn't I mention it?"

Her friend's voice was sleepy, but Georgiana's curiosity was aroused. "No. Why does he want it? From what I saw, it's terribly run down."

"Oh, it is. Run down, I mean. Even when Charles's father was alive... And now..."

Georgiana waited, but Bella's mind had clearly drifted. "But why does he want it?" she prompted.

"The Place? Oh, I keep forgetting you don't know all that much about it." Bella's skirts rustled as she sat up. "Well, you see, the Place didn't exist a hundred years ago. It used to be part of Candlewick. But one of my ancestors was something of a loose screw. He gambled heavily. One of his creditors was one of your ancestors. He agreed to take part of the Candlewick lands in payment. So that was how the Place came about. My spendthrift ancestor didn't live long, much to the family's relief. Ever since then, the family has tried to buy back the Place and make Candlewick complete again. But your family have always refused. I don't know how long it's been going on, but, generally, both families have always dealt amicably despite all. That is..." Bella paused dramatically; Georgiana sat enthralled "—until my father's death. Although he had always talked of rejoining the Place to Candlewick, my father hadn't, as far as Dominic could discover, done much about it. So when he inherited, Dominic wrote to your uncle to discuss the matter. But your uncle never replied. He was, by that time, something of a recluse. Dominic could never get to see him. After a while, Dominic gave up. When he heard of your uncle's death, he wrote to Charles. Charles didn't reply either. Mind you,'' Bella added on a reflective note, ''as Charles dislikes Dominic as much as Dominic dislikes him, I can't say I was surprised at that. Still, from what you've said, the Place is falling down about Charles's ears. I really can't see why he won't sell. Dominic's prepared to pay above the odds, and Charles must know that.''

''Perhaps it's mere stubbornness?''

''Maybe,'' Bella conceded, tiring of her brother's problems. She lapsed into silence, the better to consider the doors the evening had opened for her protégée.

Georgiana puzzled over Charles's behaviour. In the few days she'd had to observe him, her cousin had given the impression of being addicted to the good things in life, or rather, that he had a liking for the finer things but had little of the wherewithal required to pay for them. Which made his refusal to sell the Place, in which he demonstrably took no interest, stranger still.

From consideration of Charles, it was a short step to thoughts of the man so inextricably linked in her mind with her escape from her cousin. The demands of her début at Almack's had precluded her thinking of her earlier meeting with Lord Alton, beyond the wish that she had made a better impression. Undoubtedly she had appeared as a gawky, tongue-tied, awkward child. Where on earth had two years of experience gone? Certainly, nothing in her previous existence had prepared her for the odd effect he had on her. She had never reacted to a man in such a way before. It was both puzzling and unnerving. When it came to Bella's brother, her carefully nurtured Italian calm deserted her. Hopefully, by the time they next met, the peculiar effect would have worn off. She did not wish to be forever appearing as a graceless school-girl to the gentleman before whom, more than all others, she wished to shine. Still, no doubt she was refining too much on their meeting. Lord Alton would have seen her merely as a child he had assisted in her time of trouble. She could be nothing more than that to him. The thought that she would like to be a great deal more than that to Lord Alton she ruthlessly decapitated at birth. He was a noted Corinthian and, from what she had heard at the dinner-table, one of the Carlton House set. She had nothing to recommend her to his notice—not beauty, nor fortune, nor birth. To him, she would be no more than a passing acquaintance, one he had perhaps already forgotten.

Besides, it seemed he was on the verge of contracting an alliance, although Lady Winterspoon certainly seemed to think the lady in question was rather less than suitable. But she had heard more than enough in Italy to distrust the conclusions of society. Who knew? Maybe Lord Alton was genuinely fond of Lady Changley. She tried to imagine what the lady Lord Alton was in love with would look like, but soon gave up. She knew so little of him that it was impossible to guess his preferences.

As she ruminated on the twist of fate that had

caused them to meet, Georgiana reflected that it was perhaps as well she would get few chances to be in Viscount Alton's company. He was the stuff schoolgirl dreams were made of. Unfortunately, she was no longer a schoolgirl. And she did not have the capital to indulge in dreams.

CHAPTER FOUR

"MY LORD, I'm most truly sensible of the honour you do me, but, indeed, I cannot consent to becoming your wife."

Georgiana watched as Viscount Molesworth, an earnest young man more at home on his ancestral acres than in a London ballroom, rose awkwardly from his knees.

Dusting off his satin breeches, he sighed. "Thought you might say that."

Georgiana swallowed a giggle and managed to look politely interested.

Seeing this, the Viscount obligingly continued, "Told m'mother so. But you know what women are. Wouldn't listen. Said you'd be bound to accept me. Said you were just the thing I needed. Must say, I agree with her there." He glanced once more at Georgiana. "Sure you won't change your mind?"

Shaking her head, Georgiana rose and put her hand on the Viscount's sleeve. "Truly, my lord, I don't think we would suit."

"Ah, well. That's it, then." Lord Molesworth, heir to an earldom of generous proportions, lifted his head as music drifted from the ballroom down the hall. "Best get back to the dancing, then, what?"

Unable to command her voice, Georgiana nodded. Strolling back into the ballroom on his lordship's arm, she could not keep a happily satisfied smile from her face. She had known the Viscount was bordering on a declaration, had been teetering on the brink for the past week. And, as with her two previous proposals, Georgiana had dreaded having to hurt his feelings. But it had all passed off easily, even more easily than the others. Her first proposal had been from young Lord Danby, who had been truly smitten but so very young that she had felt she were dealing with a younger brother, not a potential lover. Her second offer had come from Mr Havelock, a quiet man of thirty-five summers. She was sincerely fond of him, but in a friendly way, and doubted she could ever think of him other than as a friend. He had accepted her refusal philosophically, and they continued friends, but he had impressed on her that, should she have need of support or even something more, he was forever at her disposal.

Relieved at having weathered yet another proposal with no bones broken, Georgiana gave silent thanks that she had attracted only true gentlemen. Some of the more dangerous Corinthians had certainly looked her over—almost, she had felt, as if she were a succulent morsel they were planning to gobble up. But when they learned she was staying with the Winsmeres they usually smiled and passed on.

However, there were a few who had remained long enough to enjoy a light flirtation, a moment of dalliance. Such a one was Lord Edgcombe, who now approached to claim her for the waltz.

Georgiana smiled and curtsied. "My lord."

His lordship, resplendent in a dark green coat which leant a deeper tinge to his golden locks, bowed easily over her hand. "My lovely." His cool grey eyes flicked to the Viscount, still hovering by her elbow.

Georgiana realised he must have seen them re-enter the room, and wondered how much he guessed. She was now too experienced to take umbrage at his outrageous but calculated greeting. Instead, she spoke confidently, succeeding in distracting his lordship from his contemplation of the hapless Viscount. "I take it that means you approve of my gown?"

Lord Edgcombe's grey gaze swung slowly to her face. His lips twitched. Then, to pay her back for her temerity, he raised his quizzing-glass and embarked on a minute inspection of her person. "Mmm," he murmured. "The style, of course, is superb. Fancon, I trust?"

Georgiana, far from blushing and dissolving into a twittering heap, the prescribed reaction to his behaviour, could not restrain her smile. She understood his lordship's tactics only too well.

Far from being put out by her refusal to succumb, Lord Edgcombe responded with a smile of genuine enjoyment and offered his arm. "Come, sweet torment, the dance-floor awaits and the musicians will soon grow weary."

As she twirled down the room in Lord Edgcombe's arms, Georgiana wondered again at the success, for her part unexpected but none the less flattering, which had resulted in her receiving the attentions of one such as his lordship. He was well born, with a comfortable estate, and could be pleasant enough when it suited him. However, as it only suited him to behave so with a select circle of acquaintances, he was generally thought to be beyond the reach of the matchmaking mamas. Georgiana did not entirely understand his interest in her, but instinctively knew she was in no immediate danger of receiving a proposal from Lord Edgcombe. At least, she amended, as she looked into his smiling grey eyes and correctly divined the thoughts behind them, not a proposal of marriage.

"Relieve my curiosity, my dear. What could possibly be so interesting that you needs must be alone with the noble Viscount?"

Georgiana opened her eyes wide. "Why, we were merely strolling, my lord."

The grey gaze remained on her face for a full minute. Then his lips curved once more. "I see." After a moment he added, his voice low, "I don't suppose you feel like taking a stroll with me."

Georgiana's eyes danced. Keeping her face straight, she shook her head primly. "Oh, no, my lord. I don't think that would be at all wise."

They executed a complicated turn at the end of the room, pausing to allow two younger and more enthusiastic couples to pass by. When they were once more proceeding up the long room, his lordship's attention refocused. "Now why is that, I wonder? Surely you don't mean to say that you fear my company would be less…scintillating than the Viscount's?"

Georgiana laughed lightly, her eyes still holding his. "Oh, no—far from it. My fear is more that your company might prove rather *too* scintillating, my lord."

Lord Edgcombe was no more immune to the flattery of a beautiful young woman than the next man, even if he fully understood her machinations. So he smiled again, sharing in her laughter. "My dear, you're a minx. But a delightful minx, so I'll let you escape the set-down you undoubtedly deserve."

Schooling her features to reflect a suitable gratitude, and reducing her voice to a breathless whisper, Georgiana replied, "Oh, thank you, my lord."

"Gammon!" said Lord Edgcombe.

Returning three dances later to Bella's side, Georgiana was given no time to draw breath. Her mentor immediately demanded to be told what Viscount Molesworth had had to say.

Georgiana regarded Bella warily. "He proposed."

"And?" Bella's face was alight.

Georgiana knew it was her friend's dearest wish that she contract a suitable alliance, and Viscount Molesworth was certainly that. But she had no real ambition to marry where she did not love, not even for her best friend. So she drew a deep breath and confessed. "I refused him."

"Oh." Bella's face fell. "But why?"

Seeing the real consternation in Bella's big eyes— eyes that constantly reminded her of another—Georgiana was tempted to make a clean breast of it. But the approach of the gentleman to whom she was promised for the next dance reminded her of their surroundings. "I'll explain later. Not now. Please, Bella?"

Now Bella saw Mr Millikens and smiled and nodded, adding in an undertone for Georgiana's ears only,

"Yes, of course. Later. But Georgie, we really must talk of this."

Georgiana nodded her agreement and moved forward to take Mr Millikens's arm.

The rest of the evening passed in a blur before Georgiana's eyes. She spent much of her time examining and assessing the changes the past two weeks had wrought in her life. Arthur's quietly worded request that she remain in Green Street, theoretically a guest, but in truth as a companion for Bella, had been a turning point. His explanation of Bella's need for purpose in an otherwise frivolous existence had struck a chord of sympathy. After that, she had no longer pursued the idea of finding employment with an older lady. Bella, of course, was kept in ignorance of the arrangement, for it was generally only much older women who had companions.

That first night at Almack's had set the seal on her success. From that evening, a steady flow of invitations had poured into Green Street, and she and Bella had been immersed in a tide of balls and parties, routs and breakfasts. Her popularity, both with the gentlemen and the ladies of society, had made Bella crow. For her part, Georgiana wryly thanked her less than perfect looks. Because she was no beauty, she was not a challenge to the reigning *incomparables*. Thus she was accepted without any great fuss, nor was she the butt of any jealousies. Her natural vivacity, which, thanks to Lady Winterspoon and Beau Brummel, she had discovered, carried her through. In her heart, she strongly suspected it was this, together with her unconventionally un-missish behaviour, which made her so attractive to the gentlemen. Certainly, they flocked about her. And, if she were to be truthful, she could not deny a happy little glow of self-satisfaction whenever she thought of her court. She might not be a hit, or a beauty, but she had her own little niche, her own place in the scheme of things. As Lady Winterspoon had suggested, there were many roads to success.

They were among the last to leave the ball. As she had anticipated, Bella returned to the subject of Viscount Molesworth as soon as the carriage door was shut upon them.

"Why, Georgie? I thought you liked him."

Georgiana leant back against the fine leather upholstery and resigned herself to the inevitable. "Viscount Molesworth is all that is amiable. But truly, Bella, do you think that's enough?"

"Enough? But, my dear, many girls marry with far less than—er—liking for their husbands."

Georgiana stifled a sigh. She would have to try to make Bella understand. "Bella, did you marry like that?"

Bella shifted in her seat, her satin skirts shushing. "Well, no. But…well, you know it's not the done thing, to marry for love. And," she hurried on, "you've no idea the trouble I had, in marrying Arthur. No one could understand it. Oh, it's accepted now. But if Dominic had opposed the match everyone would have agreed with him. Love is simply not a…a determining factor in marriage in the *ton*."

Hearing the sincere note in Bella's voice, Georgiana debated whether to tell her the truth. But, even as the idea formed, she shied away from it. Instead she tried another tack. "But you see, dearest Bella, I didn't come to London to marry. I've given no thought to marrying into the *ton*. I'm not at all sure it would suit me."

To this, Bella returned a decidedly unladylike snort. "Not marry? Pray tell, what else are you going to do with your life? Oh—don't tell me you'll be a companion to some old lady. You'll never convince me you would rather be that than married to some nice, considerate gentleman who'll shower you with everything you desire."

Under cover of the dark, Georgiana grinned. Well, she was a companion, although Bella didn't know it and the lady wasn't old. But would she really prefer to be married, regardless of the man, to have to tend to the comfort and consequence of some faceless gentleman? Georgiana sighed. "You make it all sound so straightforward."

"It is straightforward. It's simply a matter of making up your mind to it and then, when a suitable gentleman comes along, saying yes instead of no."

Georgiana gave a weary giggle. "Well, if the right gentleman comes along, I'll promise to consider it."

Bella wisely refrained from further pushing, hopeful that she had at least made her errant protégée think more deeply on her future position within the *ton*. For Bella was quite determined her Georgie should marry well. She was attractive, which was more to the purpose than beautiful. And the gentlemen liked her—as evidenced by three proposals within two weeks. She had held great hopes of Mr Havelock, but Georgie had refused him without a blink. All she could do now was to hope Georgie's elusive right gentleman came along before her protégée got the reputation of being difficult to please.

A GENTLE BREEZE cooled Georgiana's warm cheeks as she accompanied Lord Ellsmere back to his phaeton. She deployed her sunshade to deflect the glances of any curious passers-by as they left the secluded walk and crossed the lawns to the carriageway. Her hand resting gently on his sleeve, she cast a tentative glance up into his lordship's handsome face. He was watching her and, catching her gaze, smiled ruefully.

"Forgive me, my dear, if my actions seem somewhat importunate. You'll have to make allowances for my—er—strong feelings in this matter."

For the first time since that night at Almack's, now more than three weeks ago, Georgiana felt flustered. Only this morning she had been congratulating herself on having managed to keep her earnest suitors from making any further declarations. How could she have guessed what his lordship had planned in the guise of a perfectly decorous drive in the park?

"Oh, yes, of course," she muttered incoherently. She noticed his lordship's slightly smug expression, and her temper, usually dormant, stirred. As she allowed him to help her up to the high seat of the phaeton, she made a heroic effort to pull herself together.

She could hardly claim that no gentleman had tried to kiss her before. But, in Italy, the flowery speeches and extravagant gestures that usually preceded such an attempt gave any lady all the warning she could need, should she wish to avoid the outcome. But Lord Ellsmere had given no indication of his intent. One minute they had been strolling comfortably along a secluded walk, screened by the lush growths of a long summer from the more populated carriageway and lawns, and the next she had been trapped in his arms, quite unable to free herself—not that she had struggled, stunned as she had been. Lord Ellsmere had, unfortunately, taken her lack of reaction for acquiescence and acted accordingly. Then she had struggled.

To give him his due, Lord Ellsmere had immediately released her, only to capture her hand. He had then proceeded to declare his undying love for her, to Georgiana's utter confusion. Her mind had been miles distant before he had acted, and she had struggled to manage even the most feeble disclaimer.

And now, of course, he merely felt he had acted precipitately and swept her off her feet. He had made it clear he did not accept her refusal of his suit. He would, he had said, live in the hope she would, with time, see its advantages.

As he climbed to the seat beside her, Georgiana turned impulsively towards him. "My lord…"

Lord Ellsmere's eyes followed his diminutive tiger as the boy left the horses' heads to swing up behind them. Then he turned and smiled at Georgiana. "I'll see you at the ball tonight, my dear. We'll continue our discussion then, when you've had more time to consider."

His words were kindly, and Georgiana inwardly groaned. This was precisely the sort of situation she had been trying to avoid. But with the tiger behind, she could do nothing other than acquiesce to his lord-ship's plan.

In truth, as she felt the cooling breeze ripple past, she welcomed the time to marshal her arguments bet-ter. Lord Ellsmere was not Mr Havelock, nor Viscount Molesworth. He had every right to expect her serious consideration of his suit. He was eminently eligible— title, fortune, property and connections. Oh, heavens! What would Bella say this time?

Any thoughts Georgiana might have entertained of keeping her latest offer from her friend died a swift death when, re-entering Winsmere House, she made her way to the back parlour. Bella was there, reclining on the sofa, flicking through the pages of the latest *Ladies' Journal.* She looked up as Georgiana entered. And frowned.

"I thought you were driving with Lord Ellsmere."

Georgiana turned aside to lay her bonnet on a chair. "I was."

Bella's frown deepened. "Didn't he come in?"

"No." Georgiana would have liked to add an ex-cuse which would explain this lapse of good manners on his lordship's part, but could think of nothing to the point. Under Bella's close scrutiny, she coloured.

"Georgie! *Never* say it! He's *offered?*" Bella sat up abruptly, the magazine sliding unheeded from her lap.

Bright cheeks made it unnecessary for Georgiana to answer.

"Oh, my dear! *Ellsmere!* Whoever would have thought it? Why, he's..." Georgiana's lack of re-sponse suddenly struck Bella. She stopped in mid-exclamation, disbelief chasing elation from her face.

"Oh, no!" she moaned, falling back against the cushions. "You've *refused* him!"

Georgiana smiled weakly, almost apologetically. But she wasn't to be let off lightly. Not this time.

Half an hour later, Bella threw her hands up in the air in defeat. "But I *still* don't understand! Danby was one thing; even Mr Havelock I could sympathise with. But Molesworth…and now, of all men, Ellsmere. Georgie, you'll never live it down. No one will believe you're turning Ellsmere down for the ridiculous reason that you aren't in love with him. They'll start saying there's something wrong with you, I know they will." Bella's voice quavered on the edge of tears.

Georgiana wasn't entirely composed herself. But she endeavoured to keep her tone even as she replied, "But I don't mean to make them propose. I do everything I can think of to avoid it."

Bella frowned, aware this was so. She had watched her protégée like a hen with one chick, and had puzzled over Georgiana's apparent uninterest in her suitors as suitors, rather than acquaintances. To her mind, the offers were coming in thick and fast precisely because, in comparison with most of the other débutantes, the gentlemen found Georgie so comfortable to be with. Then the oddity in Georgiana's declaration struck her. Her head came up. "*Why* don't you wish them to become attached? You can't possibly have decided you can't love any of them. You can't expect me to believe you truly consider the single state preferable to being married."

There was no possibility of avoiding Bella's stern gaze. Georgiana had, in fact, spent the last weeks fantasising on marriage, albeit marriage to one particular gentleman. She felt her cheeks warm as she blushed guiltily.

And Bella, being Bella, and every bit as impulsive as Georgiana herself, immediately leapt to the correct conclusion. "Oh, Georgie!" she wailed. "You haven't formed a…a *tendre* for some unsuitable gentleman, have you?"

Driven to the truth, Georgiana nodded dully.

"But who?" Bella was nonplussed. She had conscientiously vetted those to whom she introduced Georgiana. There had been no one unsuitable. None of the truly dangerous blades had approached her, and, in the circles they frequented, there was precious little chance for any outsider to gain access to her charge. So who was this mysterious man?

"He's not actually unsuitable, exactly," put in Georgiana, anticipating Bella's train of thought. At her friend's interrogative glance, she looked down at her hands, clasped tightly together in her lap, and continued, "It's more a case of…of unrequited love. I fell in love with him, but he doesn't love me."

"Well, then," said Bella, perking up at this, "we'll just have to see to it that he changes his mind."

"No!" squeaked Georgiana. She drew a deep breath and went on more calmly, "You don't understand. He doesn't know I love him."

Bella looked thunderstruck. Then, after a moment, she ventured, "Well, why not tell him? Oh, not in words. But there are ways to these things, you know."

But Georgiana was adamantly shaking her head. "He's in love with someone else. In fact," she added, hoping to shut off the terrifying prospect Bella seemed set on exploring, "he's about to offer for another."

"Oh." Bella digested this unwelcome news, a frown settling over her delicate face. For the life of her, she still could not fathom who Georgie's mystery man could be. In the end, she looked again at Georgiana where she sat on a chair, twisting the ribbons of her bonnet in her fingers, an uncharacteristically desolate look in her eyes.

Bella's kind heart was touched. She had been thrilled at Arthur's scheme to hire Georgiana as her companion and truly grateful for the way Georgie had tactfully gone along with the charade. Inwardly, she vowed she would do everything possible to learn who it was who had stolen Georgie's heart and, if possible, change his mind. Unlike Georgiana, she did not imagine a man about to contract an alliance was necessarily in love with his prospective bride. Hence, she did not consider Georgie's case lost. But, if it was, she must look to protect her friend's best interests. She now knew enough of Georgiana to know she would never consider alternatives until, perhaps, it was too late. So, in a gentle way, Bella asked, "I don't mean to pry, my dear. But do you not feel you could tell me who the gentleman is?"

Georgiana hung her head. Her feelings of guilt were increasing by the minute. How could she repay Bella's kindness in this way? How could she tell Bella she was in love with her brother? Slowly she shook her head. Then, feeling some explanation was due, she said, "You know him, you see. And, as I said, he doesn't know I love him. I…think it would be unfair to tell you—unfair to you and unfair to him.''

Bella nodded understandingly. ''I won't push you, then. But perhaps, in the circumstances, it would be best if I spoke to Lord Ellsmere this evening.'' Georgiana's startled look had Bella hurrying on. ''Oh, I won't tell him what you've told me. But there are ways and means. I'll just hint him away. It would be best, I think, for all concerned if I had a word with him.''

Georgiana thought over this offer. Perhaps, in this case, she would be wise to accept Bella's superior knowledge of how things were done. She raised her eyes to her friend's blue gaze, wishing, for the umpteenth time, that Bella and her brother had taken after different parents in that respect. ''If you don't mind speaking to him…''

''Not at all.'' Bella rose and impulsively hugged Georgiana. ''Now! I'm going to ring for tea, and we'll talk about something quite different.''

Georgiana summoned a smile and tried to tell herself that the peculiar emptiness within was only hunger.

Two HOURS LATER Georgiana escaped to the sanctuary of her chamber. She did not ring for Cruickshank, wishing only to lie down and rest her aching head.

Quite when it was that she had finally realised she was in love with Lord Alton she could not be sure. Certainly, her social success and the proposals of Lord Danby and Mr Havelock had precipitated her thoughts on marriage. Only then had her feelings crystallised and gained substance. But, given that Lord Alton was so much older than she, and was shortly to marry Lady Changley, aside from having no inkling of her attachment and certainly no reciprocal emotions, she had originally decided her infatuation, for surely that was all it could be, was bound to pass. In such circumstances, and knowing Lord Alton was unlikely to spend much time in his sister's house, or dancing attendance on them, she had not seen her position as Bella's companion to be in any way compromised.

That had been before the shock of this afternoon had opened her eyes. Lord Ellsmere was all any young lady could desire. He was handsome, considerate, worldly and charming. And rich and titled... The list went on. But he was very definitely not the man she desired. When his lordship had taken her in his arms, she had been deep in a daydream in which she was walking with Bella's brother. The disappointment she had felt on realising that it was not Lord Alton kissing her had been acute.

She could no longer delude herself. What she felt for Viscount Alton was what her mother had felt for her father. She had seen them together often enough, laughing happily in a world of their own, to have an innate sense of the emotion. Love. That was what it was, plain and simple.

How had it happened?

Ridiculous it might be. Impossible it might be. But it was real.

With a great sigh, Georgiana burrowed her head into the soft pillow. How she was going to cope when next they met, as it seemed certain they would, she did not know. But cope she would. She had no intention of letting Bella guess the truth, nor of running away and leaving Bella alone. Arthur had offered her a way out of her troubles, and she had accepted in good faith. She would not let him down. Somehow she would manage.

Worn out, she closed her eyes. She needed to rest her troubled mind. And her troubled heart.

THE DUCHESS OF LEWES was holding her Grand Ball three nights later.

"One has to be a Duchess to call your ball 'Grand,'" Bella acidly remarked. "Still, one has to be seen there. It's one of the compulsory gatherings, you might say."

She had arrived in Georgiana's chamber just as that damsel emerged from her bath. Drifting to the bed, Bella fingered the lilac silk gown laid out there. Then, as if making up her mind, she turned to Georgiana. "Georgie, I know your feelings on this, but I really think you should consider wearing the sea-green gauze. You know I can never wear it. Please, wear it to please me."

Georgiana looked up, arrested in the act of towelling herself dry. Golden curls, dampened with steam, wreathed her head. For one moment she hesitated, considering Bella's plea.

"Wouldn't it cause comment, being so soon after my father's death?"

"But your father said you weren't to go into mourning, remember? And although it's common knowledge that your father has recently died, I haven't told anyone how recently. Have you?''

Georgiana shook her head. She considered the sea-green gauze. Stubbornly, she had bought three more evening gowns from Fancon, all in lilac shades, rather than wear the two gowns Bella had surreptitiously bought. But really, what right had she to refuse? It was a simple request and, after all Bella's help, it was a small price to pay. In reality, it was only her pride that forbade her to wear the delicate creations hanging ownerless in her wardrobe. So she smiled, fleetingly. ''If it would please you.''

Bella grinned happily. ''Immensely.'' Her objective gained, she did not dally but whisked off to place herself in the hands of Hills.

Some three hours later, when they had finally gained the ballroom of Lewes House, Georgiana stood beside Bella and wondered why she had not overturned her stubborn pride weeks ago. The approbation in Arthur's eyes when she had entered the drawing-room that evening had assured her that her decision to wear the gown had been the right one. And the unusually intent attention of her court, and of numerous other gentlemen she had not previously encountered, bore testimony to their approval of her change in style.

As she accepted Lord Mowbray's arm for the first waltz, she smiled happily, laughingly returning his lordship's pretty compliments. To her surprise, she had discovered she could preserve the façade of a young lady enjoying her first London Season, free of care and the tangles of love, despite her empty heart. She had never been encouraged to think her own troubles of particular note. Hence, she continued to observe the lives and foibles of those about her with interest. She treated all her court in the same friendly style she had always affected. True, there were few among the débutantes she could yet call friend, but Bella was there to supply that need, for which she would always be thankful.

Georgiana had no idea what exactly Bella had said to Lord Ellsmere. Whatever it was, he had gracefully withdrawn his suit, simultaneously assuring Georgiana of his lifelong devotion. For a whole evening, she had speculated on what Bella could have said. In the end, she decided she didn't need to know.

Despite Bella's fears, her refractory behaviour in the matter of her suitors had not given rise to any adverse effects. She was still "that most suitable Miss Hartley" to the hostesses, and the cards and invitations continued to flood in. She could hardly claim she did not enjoy the balls and parties. Yet, somewhere, some part of her was detached from it all, aloof and unfulfilled, empty and void, waiting. But, as she sternly lectured herself in the long watches of the night, what she was waiting for had no chance of arriving. Lady Winterspoon's dictum had come to her rescue. There was nothing she could do but enjoy herself, thereby pleasing Bella and, as her father would have told her, extending her own experience. So, with typical abandon, she did.

By the end of the third dance, a cotillion, the rooms were starting to fill. Georgiana was escorted back to Bella's side by her partner, Mr Havelock, and he remained beside them, chatting amiably of social happenings. When he finally made his bow and left them, Georgiana turned an impishly animated face to Bella. But what she had intended to say regarding Mr Havelock remained unsaid. In fact the words melted from her mind. Her lips parted slightly in surprise as her gaze locked with Viscount Alton's.

Dominic had made his way to Bella's side through the crush, intending to learn what had become of the golden girl he had left in her care. Only when she turned to face him did he recognise in the exquisite woodland nymph, standing slim and straight in silver-green gauze beside his sister, the same young girl whose heart-shaped face and warmed honey eyes inhabited his dreams. The realisation left him momentarily bereft of words.

It was Bella who came, unwittingly, to their rescue. She uttered a small squeal of delight and, remembering to restrain her impulsive habit of throwing her arms about his neck, grabbed both of Dominic's hands instead. He looked down at her, and the spell was broken. Smoothly, suavely, he raised her hands, first one, then the other, to his lips. "Dear Bella. Clearly in fine fettle."

"But I thought you were fixed in Brighton." Bella received her hands back, but had eyes only for her brother. She saw his gaze had moved past her to Georgiana. When he made no reply but continued to stare at Georgiana, she felt constrained to add, "But you remember Georgiana?"

"Assuredly." Dominic couldn't help himself. His voice had automatically dropped to a deeper register. He smiled into those huge honey-coloured orbs in a manner perfected by years of practice and, taking her small hand, raised it fleetingly to his lips.

Barely able to breathe, Georgiana blushed vividly and sank into the regulation curtsy.

Her blush recalled Dominic to his senses. When she straightened, his face had assumed its usual, faintly bored mien. He turned slightly to address Bella. "As you see, I've decided to exchange the extravagant but questionably tasteful entertainments of His Highness for the more mundane but distinctly more enjoyable pursuits of the *ton*."

"Shhh!" said Bella, scandalised. "Someone might hear you!"

Dominic smiled sleepily. "My dear, it's only what half of the Carlton House set are saying. Hardly fodder for treason."

Bella still looked dubious.

But Dominic's attention had wandered. "Perhaps, Miss Hartley, I can steal a waltz. Judging by the hordes of gentlemen hovering, you have few to spare."

By this time, Georgiana had regained her composure and was determined not to lose it again. "The fruits of your sister's hard work, my lord," she responded readily. She placed her hand on his lordship's sleeve, suppressing by force the shiver that ran through her at that simple contact. How on earth was she to survive a waltz?

Thankfully, Lord Alton seemed unaware of her difficulties. One strong arm encircled her waist, and she was swept effortlessly into the dance. As her feet automatically followed his lead, she relaxed sufficiently to glance up into the dark-browed face above hers.

He intercepted her glance and smiled. "So you've been filling in time with all manner of social gadding?"

Georgiana shrugged lightly. "The pleasures of the *ton* have yet to pall, though I make no doubt they eventually will."

The dark brows rose. "What a very novel point of view." Dominic's lips twitched. "Surely my sister has taught you that all débutantes must, of necessity, profess addiction to all *tonnish* pursuits?"

A small and intriguing smile lifted Georgiana's lips. "Indeed, Bella has tried to convince me of the irreparable harm my lack of long-term enthusiasm might do to my chances. Still, I prefer to hold my own views." Georgiana paused while they twirled elegantly around the end of the room, before continuing, "I find it difficult to imagine being satisfied with a routine composed entirely of balls and parties and such affairs. Surely, somewhere, there must be some greater purpose in life?"

She glanced up to find an arrested expression on the Viscount's face. Suddenly worried she had inadvertently said more than she intended, Georgiana made haste to recover. "Of course, there may be a hidden purpose in such affairs—"

"No. Don't recant." His voice was low and betrayed no hint of mirth. His eyes held hers, unexpectedly serious, strangely intent. "Your views do you credit. Far be it from me to disparage them."

Georgiana was left wondering whether there was,

underlying his seriousness, some fine vein of sarcasm she had failed to detect. But she got no chance to pursue the matter; the music ceased and Lord Alton returned her to his sister's side. With a smile and a lazy flick of one finger to Bella's cheek, and a polite inclination of his head in Georgiana's direction, he withdrew.

On the other side of the ballroom, Elaine Changley shut her ivory fan with a snap. Her cold blue eyes remained fixed upon a head of gold curls just visible through the throng. Surely Dominic hadn't left her for a schoolgirl? Impossible!

The intervening bodies shifted, and Lady Changley was afforded a full view of Georgiana Hartley, slim and elegant at Bella Winsmere's side. The blue eyes narrowed. Her ladyship had not reached her present position without learning to sum up the opposition's good points. There was no doubt the girl had a certain something. But the idea of the charms of a delicate and virginal schoolgirl competing with her own experienced voluptuousness was too ridiculous to contemplate.

Lady Changley's rouged lips set in a hard line. The thought of what her so-called friends would say if, after all her crowing, she was to lose a prize like Dominic Ridgeley to a chit of a girl fresh from the schoolroom was entirely too galling to bear. Perhaps a little reminder of what she could offer was due.

IT WAS PAST midnight when Georgiana slipped on to the terrace outside the ballroom. The last dance before supper was in progress, and the terrace was vacant except for the moonbeams that danced along its length. As the chill of the evening bit through her thin gown, she wrapped her arms about her and fell to pacing the stone flags, drawing in deep breaths of the refreshing night air.

She had yet to become fully acclimatised to the stuffy atmosphere of *tonnish* ballrooms. Feeling the heat closing in on her, she had very nearly suggested to her cavalier of the moment, Lord Wishpoole, that they retire to the terrace. Luckily, a mental vision of his lordship's face expressing his likely reaction to such an invitation had stopped her from uttering the words, and doubtless saved her from the embarrassment of extricating herself from his lordship's unnecessary and very likely scandalous company. Wary of giving Bella any further reason to view her with concern, she had pleaded a slight headache to Lord Wishpoole and headed for the withdrawing-room. Once out of his lordship's sight, she had changed direction. The long windows of the ballroom had been left ajar, but the weather had turned and few guests had availed themselves of the opportunity to stroll on the long terrace.

Georgiana leant against the low balustrade and wished she was not alone. The idea of strolling beside Lord Alton, conversing easily while they took the air, was enticing. Only, of course, there was no possibility of Lord Alton wishing to stroll with her. Unfortunately, reality and dreams did not merge in that way.

The sound of footsteps approaching one of the doors at the far end of the terrace brought her upright. Someone pulled a set of doors wide, and light spilled forth.

Startled, Georgiana looked around for a hiding-place. A tall cypress in a tub stood against the wall. Without further thought, she squeezed herself between the balustrade and the tree.

Through the scraggly branches of the tree she watched as a tall woman glided on to the terrace. The moonlight, resurrected now the doors were again shut, silvered her blonde hair. As she turned and looked towards the cypress, Georgiana caught a glimpse of diamonds glittering around an alabaster throat. The lady's silk dress clung revealingly to a ripe figure; her long, graceful arms were quite bare.

Again light flooded the terrace and was abruptly cut off. Georgiana's eyes grew round.

Dominic Ridgeley's blue eyes were hard as they rested on Elaine Changley. His brows rose. "To what do I owe the pleasure of this meeting, my lady?"

Inwardly, Elaine Changley winced at his tone. *My lady?* Clearly she had lost more than a little ground. But not a suspicion of her emotions showed on her sculpted face as she moved forward to place one slim hand on the Viscount's lapel. "Dominic, darling. Why so cold?" she purred.

To her surprise and real consternation, Lady Changley sensed an instinctive rejection, immediately suppressed, but undeniable. Shock drove her to make a grab, however unwise, for her dreams. Allowing her lids to veil her eyes, she moved seductively closer. "Surely, my love, what lies between us cannot be ended with a simple 'Goodbye'?"

Lady Changley was a tall woman. In one smooth

movement, she pressed herself to Dominic's chest, reaching up to place her lips against his.

Automatically, Dominic's hands came to her waist, initially to hold her from him. But as he felt her silken form between his hands he stopped and quite coldly considered the situation.

He had come to the terrace in response to Elaine's note, intending to make it quite clear that his "Goodbye" had meant just that. The problem he was having with Georgiana Hartley, or, rather, with making sense of his feelings towards a schoolroom chit, was his major and only concern. He had almost succeeded in convincing himself that it was merely a passing aberration, that the reason he no longer desired the company, let alone the favours, of the delectable Lady Changley was no more than a function of the natural passage of time and had nothing whatever to do with a slim form in green silk gauze. Almost, but not quite.

And now here was Elaine, providing him with a perfect chance to test the veracity of his conclusions. The acid test. Surely, if he were to kiss her now, a woman he had recently known so well, he would feel something?

On the thought, his hands moved to draw her more firmly against him. Then his arms closed around her and his head angled over hers as he took possession of her lips and then her mouth. He felt the ripple of relief that travelled through her long limbs. Warning bells sounded in his brain. He felt nothing—no glimmer of desire, no flicker of flame. The coals were long dead.

Abruptly he brought the kiss to an end and, lifting

his head, put Elaine Changley from him. "And that, my dear, is very definitely the end. Adieu and good-bye." With a terse bow, he spun on his heel.

Before he could leave, Elaine, desperate, stretched out one white hand to his sleeve. "You can't just walk away from me, Dominic. There's too much between us."

The chill of his very blue eyes as they turned on her froze Elaine Changley's blood. But, when he spoke, Dominic's voice was soft—soft and, to Elaine Changley, quite deadly. "I suspect, my dear, that you'll find you're mistaken. I should perhaps point out that any embarrassment you might suffer upon our separation will be entirely your own fault. And, fur-thermore, any attempt on your part to talk more into the relationship than was ever present will only result in your further embarrassment. So—" Dominic smiled—a singularly humourless smile—and lifted her hand from his sleeve, and thence, mockingly, to his lips "—I will, for the last time, bid you adieu."

Elaine Changley made no attempt to detain him as he strode from the terrace. She was shivering, though not from the cold. Far too experienced to run after her ex-lover, Lady Changley forced herself to stand still until her composure returned. Only then did she follow Lord Alton back into the ballroom.

Georgiana let out a long breath. She emerged from behind the tub, automatically brushing her skirt free of small sticks and needles. She felt as if she had hardly breathed since scuttling behind the tree. That, of course, was the reason she was feeling light-headed. Nothing to do with the revelation that Bella's brother

was quite clearly and indisputably in love with Lady
Changley. Why else would he have kissed her like
that? She had been too far away to overhear their conversation, or to see their expressions, but the evidence
of her eyes had been plain enough. Lady Changley
had melted into Lord Alton's arms. And he had welcomed her and kissed her as if he intended to pas-
sionately devour her.

She knew her love for him was hopeless. Had always known it.

Georgiana shivered. Slowly she looked around the
terrace. Her innocent daydream seemed more distant
than ever, elusive as the mist which wreathed the tree-
tops. With a deep sigh, she pulled open one of the
ballroom doors and re-entered the heated room. She
finally located Bella amid a knot of their friends. Pushing through the throng, she made her way to her side,
rehearsing her request to leave early on the grounds
of a headache which she could now quite truthfully
claim.

CHAPTER FIVE

DURING THE NEXT WEEK, Georgiana had plenty of opportunity to develop her tactics for dealing socially with Viscount Alton. Contrary to her expectations, his lordship graced all the functions she and Bella attended. He was politely attentive. There was nothing in his behaviour to feed the flame she was valiantly trying to dampen. To her irration, she found that fact depressing. More than ever aware of the disparity of their stations, she doggedly reminded herself that a thick skin could only be obtained through exposure. Consequently, she did not shrink from contact with Lord Alton. Instead, whenever he asked her to dance—which he invariably did at least once, and, on one memorable occasion, twice—she endeavoured to amuse him with her observations on life in the *ton*. To her surprise, he seemed genuinely entertained by her comments. Indeed, he went out of his way to encourage her to air her opinions. Doubtless, she thought, it ensured he was not overcome with boredom in her otherwise unenlivening company.

Her own motive in maintaining a steady flow of conversation lay in distracting his lordship from the other peculiar responses he awoke in her. Breathlessness, often occurring with a unnerving sense of exhilaration, was the least of these. Sometimes she believed the thudding of her heart would be plainly audible if she weren't covering the noise with her chatter. Thankfully, he had not yet noticed the tremors that ran through her at his slightest touch. She had hoped these would ease with time, with familiarity, as it were. Unfortunately, they were becoming more acute with each passing day; she went in dread of his remarking them.

Absorbed as she was with dealing with his lordship, by the time they climbed into their carriage each night to return to Green Street she was thoroughly worn out. Gradually, the strain grew, until, in order to preserve her defences for the evenings, she found herself forced to forgo the pleasures of the day. When she excused herself from the afternoon's promenade for the second day in a row, Bella's concern became overt.

"Georgie, I simply cannot bear to see you so pulled down." Bella plumped herself down on the *chaise-longue* beside her friend. Georgiana was listlessly plying her needle, setting the occasional stitch in a piece of fine embroidery. Bella glanced anxiously into her face. "You aren't going into a decline, are you?"

Despite her tiredness, Georgiana grinned. "Of course not." After a moment she added, "I assure you I've no intention of pining away. It's just that I find the...the tension of the evening entertainments draining."

Born and bred to such things, Bella could not readily imagine being drained by a ball. However, she was not without sympathy. She frowned as she mulled over the matter. "We could cut down a trifle, perhaps. The

Minchintons' ball is on Friday—we need not go to that, I suppose."

But curtailing Bella's activities because of her own weakness was further than Georgiana was prepared to go. She was supposed to be Bella's companion, not an inhibiting influence. "Don't be a goose," she replied, her tone affectionate but firm. "I'm only feeling a bit low, that's all. I dare say if I make a special effort I'll be fine by this evening." She paused. "On second thoughts, perhaps some fresh air would help. If you'll wait, I'll get my bonnet and come with you."

"Of course." Bella smiled encouragingly.

But as soon as Georgiana disappeared through the door, the frown return to Bella's face. Far from reassuring her, Georgiana's rapid about-face convinced her that her friend was endeavouring, however unsuccessfully, to conceal the true effect of her hopeless love. Who knew to what depths of misery Georgie descended when no one was by? Bella fretted over the problem, rendered more acute by the restraint she felt in confiding in anyone. Arthur was her long-time mentor, but in this case Bella felt she would need Georgiana's permission before revealing her friend's state to him.

Georgiana's footsteps sounded in the hall. With a sigh, Bella rose and picked up her discarded bonnet, absent-mindedly swinging it by its long aqua ribbons. She sorely needed advice. Then, in one instant of blinding clarity, she saw the answer. Dominic. He knew all of Georgiana's background. And, after all, Georgiana herself had seen fit, at the very outset, to confide in him.

When Georgiana stuck her head around the door, Bella grinned widely. "Yes, I'm coming," she called and, feeling much more light-hearted, all but tripped from the room.

"PLEASE, DOMINIC. I really *must* talk to you. Privately." Bella put every ounce of sisterly need into her gaze as it rested on her brother's handsome face. But his habitually bored mask showed no evidence of lifting. In fact, she noted, he regarded her even more dubiously than he had before her plea.

"I warn you, Bella, I need no lectures from you."

Far from striking fear into her heart and stifling her request as intended, his precise tones made her relax and give a dismissive smile.

"Not about that! I want to talk to you about Georgiana."

"Oh!" Dominic followed her gaze to the object of their discussion, twirling gaily about the dance-floor in Harry Edgcombe's arms. Then the piercingly blue eyes swung back to Bella. "What about Miss Hartley?"

Bella looked at the knots of people surrounding them. "Not here." She glanced impishly up at him. "Don't you know of an alcove where we might be alone?"

The blue eyes glinted down at her. "Don't be impudent." He caught her hand and drew it through his arm. "As it happens," he said, leading her through the crowd, "I do. But I can't spare too many minutes. I'm engaged to dance with Miss Hartley myself, two dances hence."

"It won't take long," Bella promised.

The small ante-room Dominic led her to was thankfully empty. She sank on to a well padded sofa. Dominic elected to stand, leaning one blue-silk-clad arm along the mantelpiece. "Perceive me all ears, dear sister."

Bella eyed him suspiciously, but could detect no hint of the sarcasm he frequently employed when irritated. "As I said, it's about Georgiana." Now she came to it, she found herself short of the necessary words.

"Has she discovered Arthur's little deception and become difficult?"

"No, no. Nothing like that." Bella frowned, then, sensing Dominic's growing impatience, she abandoned her efforts to find the best phrasing and blurted out, "She's fallen in love."

For a moment, she wondered whether he had heard. His face showed no reaction to her words; he seemed frozen, petrified. Then his black brows rose. "I see." He turned aside, resetting the fine lace on his cuff. "It is, after all, not an uncommon happening. Who is the lucky man?"

"That's just it. She won't say."

Dominic's eyes rested thoughtfully on his sister's dark head. "And you imagine, as she won't divulge his name, he must therefore be in some way unsuitable."

"No, that's not it either." Bella glanced up to find her brother's eyes full on her, irritation fermenting in their blue depths. She hastened to explain. "He's not unsuitable in the way you mean. But it seems she's fallen *irrevocably* in love with a man who's about to offer for another. She says he doesn't know she's in love with him. I've tried to get her to confide in me, but she won't. She says I know him so it wouldn't be fair.''

Dominic digested this information in silence. Then, abruptly, he pushed away from the mantelpiece and paced across the room. Returning, he looked again at his sister. ''How, then, am I supposed to help? I do take it I'm supposed to help?''

Bella smiled, a trifle warily. ''Yes, of course. I wouldn't have told you if I didn't think you could help. I want you to find out who Georgie's gentleman is.''

Dominic's brows flew. ''That all?''

At his tone, Bella's face fell. ''But you must be able to guess. Who is it whom I know is about to marry? Or at least offer for someone. You men always know such titbits before it's common knowledge.''

Pacing once more, Dominic considered his acquaintance. He knew all the gentlemen his sister was on speaking terms with, and would very likely know if any were contemplating matrimony. ''Unfortunately, to my knowledge, no one fits the bill.''

Twisting her fingers anxiously, Bella ventured, ''I had wondered whether it was Lord Edgcombe.''

''Harry?'' Dominic paused, then shook his head. ''Not likely. He does have to marry in the not overly distant future or risk his family hauling him to the altar themselves. But he must marry money, and I doubt Miss Hartley's prospects fit his bill.''

"But couldn't she have fallen in love with him anyway? He's certainly personable enough."

Again, Dominic gave the matter his consideration. Again, he shook his head. "Harry has no plans to marry yet awhile. I doubt he'd even mention the possibility to a young lady circumstanced as Miss Hartley is. And, certainly, he would not have suggested he's about to do the deed." He uttered a short laugh. "Not even to escape a snare would Harry bring up the subject of marriage."

Bella sighed. "So you can't guess either." Disheartened, she stood and shook out her skirts.

Dominic hadn't moved from his stance in the middle of the floor. Now he looked shrewdly at Bella. "What prompted you to ask for help?"

Bella shrugged. "It's just that Georgie's so wan and listless nowadays."

"Listless?" her brother echoed, the vision of Miss Hartley as he had last seen her vivid in his mind. "I've rarely seen anyone *less* listless."

"Oh, not in the evenings. She seems quite lively then. But during the day she's drawn and quiet. Her looks will suffer if she goes on as she is. If *only* she would accept Mr Havelock."

"Havelock? Has he offered for her?"

Bella frowned at the odd note in her brother's voice. It was not like Dominic to be so insultingly disbelieving. "Yes," she averred. "Not only Mr Havelock, but Lord Danby and Viscount Molesworth. *And* Lord Ellsmere, too!"

For once, she had the satisfaction of knowing she

had stunned her brother. Dominic's brows rose to astronomical heights. "Good lord!"

After a moment, his puzzled gaze swung back to her face. "And she refused them all? Even Julian?"

Bella nodded decisively. "Even Lord Ellsmere." She looked down at her hands, clasped schoolgirl fashion before her. "I don't know what I'm to do, for there's bound to be more offers. They can't seem to help themselves."

She looked up to see her brother's shoulders shaking. Bella glared. "It's not funny!"

Dominic waved one white hand placatingly. "Oh, Bella! Would that all women had a sense of humour like Miss Hartley's. I assure you she would see the oddity in such a situation."

Bella was puzzled by her brother's far-away smile. But before she drummed up enough courage to ask what prospect it was that so fascinated him, he came back to earth. "And, speaking of Miss Hartley, we must, I'm afraid, return to the ballroom."

Falling into step beside him, Bella tucked her hand in his arm. "You will try to discover who he is, won't you?"

Dominic's eyes glinted steely blue. "Fear not, Bella mine. I'll give it my most earnest consideration."

And with that Bella had perforce to be content.

IT WAS WELL AFTER midnight when Dominic returned to Grosvenor Square. He let himself in with his latchkey. In the large tiled hall, shadows danced about a single candle burning in a brass holder on the central table. He had long ago broken his staff of their preferred habit of lying in wait for him to return from his evening entertainments. Picking up the candle, he stood at the foot of the stairs, contemplating the broad upward sweep. Then he turned aside and made for a polished door to one side of the hall.

The fire in the library was a glowing mass of coals. He lit the candles in the large candelabrum on the mantelpiece before crouching to carefully balance a fresh log on the embers. After a little encouragement, the flames started to lick along the dry wood.

Standing, he stretched, then crossed to the sideboard. A balloon of fine brandy in one hand, he returned to the wing-chair by the fireplace and settled his cold feet on the fender.

Georgiana Hartley. Undoubtedly the most beguiling female he had met in over a decade on the town. And she was in love with another man. Furthermore, she was in love with a man who didn't even have the good sense to love her. Ridiculous!

Dominic stared into the flames. For what felt like the six hundreth time, he tried to make himself believe that his interest in Miss Hartley didn't exist. But he had travelled that road before and had given up weeks ago. What he had yet to discover was what his interest in Georgiana Hartley portended.

He couldn't believe it was love. Not after all these years. His experience of the opposite sex was as extensive as hers was negligible. And he had never felt the slightest inclination to succumb to any of the proffered lures. Why on earth should he suddenly wish to entangle himself with a young woman barely free of the schoolroom?

Yet he could not get her out of his mind. Her heart-shaped face and honey-gold eyes inhabited his thoughts to the exclusion of almost everything else. He had underestimated the strength of his distraction when he had returned from Candlewick to Brighton. The chit had unexpected depths. Her eyes, like a siren's song, beckoned with a promise he found difficult to resist. Luckily he had realised his state before Elaine had precipitated any renewal of their intimacy. She had, predictably, reacted badly to his withdrawal.

Light from the flames gilded the spines of the leather-covered tomes on the shelves which stretched away into darkness on either side of the fireplace. Dominic took a sip of his brandy, then sank his chin into his cravat, cradling the glass between his hands. He had no regrets about Elaine. In truth, his desire for her had waned before the advent of Georgiana Hartley had banished all thought of illicit dalliance from his mind. A smile of gentle malice touched his lips. Doubtless Elaine would suffer due embarrassment as a result of her posturing. It had been her plan to use public knowledge of their relationship to pressure him into making her aspirations come true. She had been most indiscreet. Lionel, Lord Worthington, his guardian prior to his attaining his majority, had even been moved to post to Candlewick to dissuade him from contracting a *mésalliance,* on account of the bluster of a trollop's long tongue. No, he had no sympathy for such as Elaine Changley.

The fire crackled and hissed as the fresh log settled. With a sensation akin to relief, he turned his mind from the past to contemplate the nebulous future. What did his feelings for Georgiana Hartley mean? Did they amount to anything more than infatuation, regrettable but harmless and, most importantly, transient? Would the lovely Georgiana fade from his mind in six months' time, as Elaine Changley had? These were the questions that tormented him. They had forced him to return to London, to assuage a need he did not wish to acknowledge. Yet, after a week in the capital, he was no nearer the answers.

The only truth he had uncovered was that his normally even temperament was now somehow dependent on Miss Georgiana Hartley's smile.

He dropped his head back against the deeply padded leather. He had tried to tell himself she was too young, little more than a schoolgirl. Any liaison between them would be virtually cradle-snatching. But, whenever he thought along such lines, Arthur's and Bella's happiness would rise up to mock him. And, even worse, Georgiana no longer *looked* like a schoolgirl. Every time they met, Fancon's gowns, or, rather, the delectable shape they displayed, shredded his well rehearsed rationalisations.

But enough was enough. According to Bella, Georgiana was making herself ill over some no-hoper. He had no right to intervene. Not, that was, unless he wished to take their interaction further, to make some positive move in her direction. And that, he was not yet prepared to do.

If Bella, or anyone else, got a whiff of his possible intentions, there would be no chance of wooing her in private. Their every meeting would be watched over by dozens of gimlet eyes. Every word, every expression would be duly noted and analysed. He couldn't subject her to that, not when he wasn't sure what he wanted of her.

Experience, however, was on his side. If he wished, he did not doubt he could create the necessary opportunities to advance his cause, without alerting every gossip-monger in the *ton*. He smiled. There was an undeniable challenge in such an enterprise. The snag was, he was not yet sure. Not sure of what he felt for her. Not sure of what he would do once he was certain the odd feeling in his chest was more than infatuation.

It had taken him three weeks to reach his present state of acknowledged indecision. He had no intention of enduring the situation for much longer, particularly if Georgiana threatened to pine away before his very eyes. Still, how did one test an infatuation? Never having suffered such an emotion before, he had no real idea how to proceed.

The clock in the corner ticked ponderously, marking his heartbeats. His eyes grew unfocused as he stared at the flames slowly dying around the charred log. Finally he stirred. He drained his glass, then rose to return it to the tray. He relighted his bedroom candle at the candelabrum, then snuffed the five long candles it held. In the soft flickering light of the single flame, he made his way to the door.

If he wanted to burn out his obsession with Georgiana Hartley, there was only one way to go about it. He needed to meet with her often, in every possible context, to see all her faults and blemishes, the little incompatibilities which would reduce her status in his mind to one of a mere acquaintance. That was the only way forward.

And, if it proved to be more than infatuation, it was high time he faced up to the truth. And acted.

"I TOLD YOU everyone would be here." Bella stopped on the lawn below the terrace. Tucking her furled parasol under one arm, she retied the strings of her new bonnet in a jaunty bow beneath one ear. "Lady Jersey's entertainments are always well attended, particularly when they're held here."

"Here" was Osterley Park, and the entertainment in question was an alfresco luncheon. To Georgiana, standing patiently by her friend's side, it seemed as if the entire *ton* was gathered on the manicured lawns sloping gently away from the Palladian mansion to the shrubberies and parkland beyond. "Lady Lyncombe is nodding to us. Over there on the left."

Bella turned and bowed politely to the portly matron, who had three gangling girls in tow. "Poor dear. Freckle-faced, the lot of them. She'll never get them off her hands."

Georgiana stifled a giggle. "Surely it can't be that bad. They might be quite nice young girls."

"They can be as nice as they please, but they'll need something more to recommend them to the eligible gentlemen." Bella sighed, in keeping with her worldly-wise pose.

Strolling by her side, Georgiana wondered what it was that recommended her to the gentlemen. Certainly not her looks, for, in her estimation, these were only passing fair. And her fortune was, she suspected, so small as to be negligible. Yet she had received four offers. Despite the fact that she had wished to avoid each one, the very existence of four eligible offers was no small fillip to her confidence.

Smiling and bowing to acquaintances, they strolled the length of the lawn to where three gaily striped marquees had been erected. One housed the beverages; one protected the food. The third was a withdrawing-room of sorts, where ladies feeling the effects of the sun could rest before rejoining the crush.

And it certainly was a crush. The broad expanses were filled with swirling muslins and starchy cambrics, parasols and elegantly cut morning coats dotting the colourful scene. It was difficult to see more than ten feet in any direction. Registering this fact, Georgiana turned to Bella to point out the advisability of staying close together. Too late.

"If you're looking for Bella, she's fallen victim to Lady Molesworth."

Georgiana looked up into Viscount Alton's blue eyes. He was smiling, and she noted the set of small lines radiating from the corners of his eyes. Such a handsome face. Entranced, she forgot her role of sister's companion and smiled warmly back.

Dominic expertly captured her hand and conveyed it to his lips. He caught his breath when she smiled with such guileless joy. For one instant, he could almost believe...

A sudden intentness in Lord Alton's gaze brought Georgiana to her senses. "Oh! Er—where exactly?" She flustered and blushed, and turned away as if looking for Bella, to cover her confusion.

"No, no. This way." Dominic's voice was gentle, softened by an emotion he couldn't quite define.

Georgiana looked where he indicated—to the right—and found Bella deep in discussion with Lord Molesworth's mother—she who had decreed Georgiana could not do other than marry her son.

Dominic recalled Bella's mention of the luckless Viscount. His grin grew. "Perhaps," he said, "as Bella is so absorbed, I could escort you on a ramble by the lake. It's really much more pleasant than being packed amid all this crowd. Unless you're famished?" One black brow rose interrogatively.

"Oh, no," Georgiana disclaimed. She bit her lip. The prospect of a stroll in less cramped surroundings was very tempting. But could she weather such an excursion with Lord Alton? Were her nerves up to it? She glanced up at him and found him regarding her quizzically, as if trying to read her mind. As she watched, a faintly satirical gleam entered the very blue eyes, and his brows rose slightly, as if in challenge. Puzzled, she put aside her misgivings. "If it wouldn't be too boring for you."

With a laugh, Dominic offered her his arm. When she laid one small hand on his sleeve, he covered it with his other hand. "My dear Miss Hartley—or can I call you Georgiana?" He felt the hand under his quiver. His brows rose again. He looked down into her golden eyes. "Oh, yes. Surely, in the circumstances, I can claim that privilege?"

Georgiana had no idea how she should answer. But her nerves were already a-tingle, and she didn't have the capacity to cope with distractions. So she merely inclined her head in assent. "If it pleases you, my lord."

Oh, it pleased him. In fact Dominic felt inordinately pleased with that small success. "As I was saying, my dear Georgiana," he continued, deftly steering her clear of Lord Harrow, another of her present encumbrances, "your company is forever entertaining. Tell me, which of your suitors do you favour?"

Now what on earth was she to answer to that? Georgiana thought quickly, then assumed a bored air. "Why, in truth, I'd not given the matter much thought, my lord." She heard a deep chuckle. "It's all so fatiguing, this marriage game." Lassitude dripped from her every syllable.

Laughing, he countered, "Very neat, my dear. But don't let any of the *grandes dames* hear you espousing such controversial standards. You'll be driven forth, cast out from the bosom of the *ton*."

Georgiana smiled, dropping her pose. "In all honesty, I'm not sure I'm suited to this life."

To mock her words would be the easy way out. Instead Dominic answered seriously. "My dear, it's such as you who keep the *ton* alive."

Her eyes flew to his face.

Reading the question in the golden-lit depths, he explained, "If we did not have people with different ideas, people brought up to different ideas, such as yourself, join us now and then, to refresh our tired fashions, then the *ton* would be an excessively boring and stale society. Instead, if you look about you carefully, you'll see the *ton* encompasses a wide spectrum of tastes and types." He smiled down at her. "Don't worry. You'll fit in. You'll eventually find your place, that niche that has your name engraved on it.''

Shyly Georgiana returned his smile.

They strolled on in companionable silence, around the shrubberies and on to the shore of the lake. A cool breeze lifted off the expanse of grey-green water, flicking little wavelets across the surface. Beeches lined an avenue that followed the bank, golden leaves a carpet beneath the still canopied crowns. There were other guests enjoying the peace, but none intruded on their privacy.

While enjoying the early autumn colours, Georgiana pondered the cause of his earlier satirical look. As she noted the giggling and sighing of more than one damsel they passed, it suddenly occurred to her that Lord Alton might have thought she was questioning the propriety of walking alone with him. Inwardly, she sighed. If only that were her trouble. But she was abysmally aware she was in no danger of receiving any amorous attentions from Bella's brother. Rather, she was more afraid of boring him witless. She cast about in her mind for a suitable topic of conversation.

Far from being bored, Dominic was revelling in the unusual pleasure of strolling in relative peace in a glorious setting with a beautiful woman who was blessedly silent. The only itch to his contentment was the realisation of how deeply contented he in fact was. That, and the strength of his desire to preserve the moment at whatever cost. That unnerved him.

''Do you spend much time with the Prince Regent? What's he like?''

Georgiana's questions broke his train of thought.

Dominic paused, considering, before he answered. ''My family have for the past few generations been close to the throne.'' He smiled down at her. ''In the present case, the Regent.''

''But...'' Georgie hesitated. She had taken in enough of the discussion between Lord Alton and Arthur over Bella's dinner-table to realise the Viscount was more deeply involved in politicking than one might suppose from his pose of arrogantly bored aristocrat. Carefully choosing her words, she ventured, ''You discuss politics with His Highness, don't you? Not just...well, social matters.''

Inwardly cursing Arthur for his lapse from their normal secretiveness, Dominic attempted to turn her far too perceptive query aside. He laughed lightly. ''I assure you, my dear, that—er—social matters are generally dominant with the Regent.''

The teasing look he sent her along with his words should have had her blushing. Instead, he saw her beautiful eyes narrow slightly, and knew his diversion had failed. Damn it! She was younger than Bella. She should accept his word without question. And since when did young ladies institute probing inquisitions into a man's politics? She deserved a set-down. Instead, Dominic heard himself say, ''However, you're quite right. I do act as a sort of...conduit—a channel of communication, if you like—between certain factions of the Parliament and the Regent.'' He paused to help her step over a large tree root distorting the even surface of the path. Settling her hand once more in the crook of his arm, he continued, ''Despite appearances, Prinny is not entirely insensitive to the problems of the realm. And, while he has limited powers as far as actual law-making goes, his influence can go a long way to seeing changes made where they are desperately needed.''

''And you explain these things to him?''

Dominic laughed. ''Oh, no! I merely act as a form of Greek messenger.''

Georgiana looked her question. Smiling, he explained. ''My task is merely to bring up the subject, to introduce the problem, whatever it might be, to His Highness's notice.'' He grinned. ''That's why I'm back from Brighton with leisure to enjoy your company.''

Georgiana frowned, puzzling this out. ''He didn't like your last problem?''

Her companion's gaze had shifted to the distance, but he was still smiling.

''Not in the least. I'm presently in disgrace, although, of course, that's not general knowledge.''

It seemed to Georgiana that there was quite a deal about the fascinating Viscount that was not general knowledge. But before she could frame any further questions, they emerged from the beech walk and were joined by a gaggle of young ladies and their escorts. Viscount Molesworth was there; so too was Lord Ellsmere. Georgiana caught a look of surprise on Lord Ellsmere's handsome face, followed swiftly by an expression she could only interpret as consideration. However, he said nothing to her, beyond a polite greeting, and fell into step on the other side of Lord Alton, engaging the Viscount in a low-voiced conversation which seemed to have a distinctly pugilistic flavour. In a laughing, chattering group, they made their way back to the marquees. Bella met them there. To Georgiana's disappointment, she got no further chance to converse alone with Lord Alton.

TWO NIGHTS LATER, a masked ball was to be held at Hattringham House. Bella was thrilled. "It's quite fun, really. Most people know who you are, of course, but the masks allow everyone to pretend they don't."

It was the afternoon of the big event, and Bella was lolling on Georgiana's bed.

Georgiana was frowningly considering her wardrobe. The one evening dress she had yet to wear was the topaz silk. For some reason, she had resisted temptation, saving it for some undefined purpose. She rather thought the time for wearing it had come. Why she should feel so she had no idea. She simply did. She drew it forth and held it to her.

"Oooh, yes!" said Bella, bouncing up. "I'd forgotten about that one. It's perfect."

"You don't think it's a little too…?" Georgiana gestured vaguely.

"Heavens, no! A 'little too…' is exactly what one wants for a masked ball."

"Do you have a mask I can borrow?"

"Heaps! They're in a drawer in my room." Bella sat up and jumped off the bed. "Come, let's go and look. Bring the dress."

Five minutes later they had found the mask. A bronzed affair with elaborate upswept wings, it fitted snugly across Georgiana's upper face from forehead to upper cheeks. Her hazel eyes glittered from the darkened depths of the slanted eye holes. There was no debate on the matter; it was perfect.

When they descended the stairs that evening to twirl joyfully about Arthur in the hall, his face told them they were both visions of delight. "You won't be able to move for all the beaux at your feet," he said, taking one hand of each fair maid and gallantly bestowing a kiss on them both.

As he escorted his two charges to their carriage, Arthur smiled in fond anticipation. He was accompanying them ostensibly because the Hattringham House ball was one of the major events of the Season. In reality, he cared little for the social swim but intended to keep a watchful eye on his youthful wife. Bella too often forgot that what she intended as innocent play might be reciprocated by actions far from innocent. As he rarely had time to devote solely to his wife, Arthur was looking forward to enjoying the evening. He knew Dominic would be there and was quite sure he could leave his brother-in-law to look after Georgiana. In fact, he thought, as his gaze rested on the alluring figure clad in topaz silk seated opposite, he doubted his brother-in-law, in his present state, would have eyes for anyone else.

Georgiana travelled the miles to Hattringham House in an unusual state of nervous anticipation. Nervous anticipation of itself was no surprise—she was accustomed to feeling it grow every time she appraoched the moment she would meet Bella's brother. But tonight the tension was heightened. It was the fault of the dress. If she had known how it would affect her, she would never have worn it. Far from decreasing her anxiety, the realisation tightened the knots in her stomach. Inwardly quivering with trepidation, she accepted Arthur's hand to descend from the carriage to the torchlit steps of Hattringham House. With assumed calm, she glided beside Bella as they made their way through the hall and into the ballroom beyond.

There was no footman to announce anyone, of course. The guests merely entered and joined the shifting throng. Already the rooms were crowded. Glittering jewels winked under the chandeliers. Gay silks and satins swirled, fans fluttered in flirtation, curls bobbed teasingly about artful faces. A hubbub of conversation rose to swamp them; warm air redolent with a heady mix of perfumes and flower scents wrapped them about.

"Phew! What a crush!" exclaimed Bella. "And it's not even ten."

A tall, dark-haired gentleman materialised at Georgiana's side. He bowed elegantly over her hand. "Could I beg the favour of this dance, fair maid?"

Behind the dark mask, Georgiana descried the features of Lord Ellsmere. "I would be honoured, my lord," she replied, rising from her curtsy.

"Now how do you know if I'm a lord or not?" her partner asked as he whirled them on to the floor.

"Given that at least half the gentlemen present must be titled, it seemed a reasonable assumption," Georgiana glibly explained. "And besides, even if wrong, the mistake could only flatter, whereas, if it were the other way about, I could be stepping on toes."

His lordship laughed. "You never step on my toes, my dear."

Abruptly Georgiana wondered whether he had accepted her dismissal of his suit or was, in reality, merely waiting in the expectation that she would change her mind. Held easily within his arm, she was loweringly conscious that she felt nothing—no ripple of excitement, no increase in her heartbeat to betray her emotions. His nearness touched her not at all.

The dance ended and they whirled to a halt. Immediately they were mobbed by a crowd of gentlemen, all wishful of securing a dance with the exciting newcomer. Not everyone recognised her; of that Georgiana was certain. But before she could make sense of all their requests and determine whom it was safe for her to accept, a deep voice spoke from just beside her.

"My claim is first, I think."

Georgiana glanced up, her breath trapped, as usual, somewhere between her lungs and her throat. Her eyes took in the tall, broad-shouldered form at her side, exquisitely garbed, dark hair falling in waves about a dark mask. Blue, blue eyes watched her from the depths of the mask. Even if his eyes and voice hadn't informed her clearly who he was, her senses were screaming it.

"Of course, my lord," she said, drawing again on her inner strength, the only way she could weather the storm of emotions his nearness always unleashed within her. She placed her hand on his proffered arm and allowed him to lead her on to the floor, entirely forgetting the rest of her court.

"Well!" expostulated Viscount Molesworth, left standing by Lord Ellsmere. "If that don't beat the Dutch!" He glared at the broad shoulders of the gentleman whose arms now held the lady in topaz silk. His glare turned to a petulant frown. "Who is he, anyway?"

Lord Ellsmere was watching the couple on the dance-floor, a slight smile on his face. He looked down at the Viscount. "Don't you know?"

Lord Molesworth puffed indignantly. "Wouldn't ask if I did. Stands to reason."

Julian Ellsmere continued to watch the dancers, then, shaking his head in wonderment, left Lord Molesworth without his answer.

Georgiana was struggling to subdue her senses, running riot as usual. As they reached the end of their first circuit, she felt almost in control again. If Lord Ellsmere left her cold, Lord Alton did exactly the opposite. She felt flushed—all over. And the peculiar sensation of weakness she had suffered during their more recent meetings seemed tonight to be intensified. Perhaps it was because he was holding her rather more closely than was the norm. Still, at least her brain seemed to be functioning again.

If she had been more experienced, Georgiana might have wondered at her partner's silence. But, engrossed in her inner struggle, she did not question what it was that kept Lord Alton speechless for the better part of the waltz. Dominic was, in fact, dealing with a revelation of his own. When he had seen Georgiana enter the ballroom at Bella's side her beauty had stunned him to immobility. In his eyes, she was the most ravishing female in the room. A goddess, all gold and bronze. A golden angel, from the topmost gold curl to the tip of her tiny gold slippers. A prize beyond price.

He had watched as she circled the floor in Julian's arms, dazedly waiting until he could approach her. He no longer questioned the effect she had on him; it was now too marked to ignore. But, as he had deftly extricated her from her other admirers, for the first time his full attention had been focused on her. What he saw had effectively knocked him back on his heels. He was far too experienced not to recognise the signs. In all their previous meetings, his mind had been fully occupied in analysing his responses to her, not her responses to him. Now, all his well honed expertise on alert, he let his senses feel for her, and convey back to him her state. Every little move she made was now registered—every indrawn breath, every flicker of an eyelid. The information came in and was automatically assessed, allowing him to respond to her smoothly, easily, encouraging her, heightening her awareness of him, learning her reactions to his attentions. His instinctive conclusions hammered at his conscious mind. When had it happened? In truth, he didn't care. All that now concerned him was how to capture what was there, how to foster and nurture her feelings, to make them grow to what he desired them to be. And all his experience told him that wouldn't be difficult.

So, with gentle patience, he waited until she had herself in hand once more and could cope with his, "And what might your name be, fair one?"

Georgiana blinked. Surely he recognised her? But then, she reflected, she wasn't sure the others had either. Maybe it wasn't that obvious. She thought quickly, then replied, "I really don't think the purpose of her ladyship's entertainment would be furthered if I answered that question, my lord.''

Inwardly, Dominic grinned, but outwardly he was all dejection. "But what, then, should I call you, sweetheart?''

It was a struggle to keep her tone even. "'Sweet-heart' will do very nicely, my lord.''

Great heavens! Had she really said that? Georgiana glanced up from under her long lashes and blushed when she encountered her partner's blue gaze. But he merely smiled, slowly, and said, "Sweetheart it is, then, my dear.''

His deep voice sent tingling shivers down her spine. What on earth was she doing? What on earth was he doing?

The music ceased, and Georgiana turned towards the other end of the ballroom, where she had left Bella. Her partner detained her by the simple expedient of tightening the arm that still lay about her waist. "Oh, no, sweetheart,'' he said on a soft laugh. "Hasn't any-one told you?'' At her enquiring look, he explained, "One of the main—if not the primary—purposes of a *balle masquée* is to permit those who wish to…further their acquaintance to do so without attracting the no-tice of the tattle-mongers.'' His voice had dropped to a mesmerising tone. His breath wafted the curls about her ear as he bent closer to add, "And I find I very definitely want to further my acquaintance with you.''

Georgiana gasped. There was no doubting the subtle invitation couched in those otherwise innocuous words. Involuntarily, her eyes sought his in the dark-ened recesses of his mask. The glow she saw in the blue depths merely served to tighten the iron band that had clamped around her chest, threating to suspend her breathing. "My lord!"

Despite her panic, her words came out in a seductive whisper, quite contrary to her intention. It was as if something stronger than her will was impelling her to accept the challenge she saw in his eyes.

He laughed, softly, his eyes on hers, and Georgiana's bones felt weak. Then he put the challenge into words. "Surely, sweetheart, you're not afraid of what you might learn?"

His head was bent close to hers, his large body overwhelmingly near. His breath felt warm against her cheek; his hands came up to surreptitiously stroke her arms where they were bare above her elbow-length gloves. Georgiana could not repress the shiver of pure delight that coursed through her at his touch.

What on earth was he doing? Dominic mentally sat at a distance and marvelled at himself. He knew— none better—that this was no way to behave towards a gently reared young lady. To experienced courtesans, to the likes of Elaine Changley, his attentions would be perfectly in order. But delicate virgins were apt to flee for cover, to faint or screech if treated to such subtle but strong tactics. Certainly, they wouldn't know how to respond to them. The trouble was, Georgiana Hartley's responses had more in common with those of a courtesan than of the virgin he knew her to be. Fascinated, he waited for her reaction.

Georgiana had no thought of fleeing, fainting or screeching. Her conscious mind was entirely taken up with a fight against her desire to learn what it was his lordship proposed to teach her. Desire won, hands down. She'd deal with reality later.

"Afraid?" she echoed, buying time. "Hardly that. But I do wonder at the wisdom of being seen too much together. Surely our friends, if no one else, will recognise us and think it odd?"

Dominic understood the hidden meaning in her words, but chose to ignore it. He was in no hurry to confirm or deny his recognition of her. "In this mêlée? I doubt any of our friends can even see us. Can you see any of your party?"

He had already seen Bella and Arthur move into one of the adjoining salons, so was not surprised when, after a quick survey of the room, Georgiana shook her head. "I can't see anyone I know."

Smiling, Dominic tucked her hand into his arm. "You see? A *balle masquée* is a time to have fun. So come and enjoy yourself with me." As he steered her in the direction of the terrace, he added for her ears only, "I assure you I have every intention of enjoying myself with you."

To Georgiana's delight, the evening proved to be one of unalloyed pleasure. Initially, she was wary, convinced Lord Alton had not recognised her, and on tenterhooks lest he, not knowing who she was, overstepped the line. Instead, while he certainly drifted very close to the invisible limit of acceptable conduct, he never once gave her cause to rue her deception. For deception it certainly was. What on earth would he think if he ever learnt it was his sister's little protégée on whom he was lavishing his attentions?

To be the object of his attentions was a most sinful

pleasure. Georgiana sparkled, animated as she had not been since her father's death. For one blissful evening she forgot her situation, forgot her cousin, forgot everything beyond the dancing lights in a pair of cerulean blue eyes. They walked through the salons and he pointed out numerous well known identities hidden behind their masks, elaborating on their idiosyncrasies, regaling her with gossip and the latest *on dits,* making her laugh, making her blush. When she confessed to hunger, they found the supper-room and helped themselves to heaps of lobster patties. She had her first taste of champagne, and giggled as it fizzled down her throat. They danced again, waltzing with effortless grace. Georgiana felt as if she were floating, held to earth by the strong clasp of his arm about her waist, drawn to heaven by the warmth in his eyes. Later they strolled on the terrace. She stood at the balustrade and he stood behind her, pointing out the features of the famous topiary gardens, thrown into silvered relief by the moonlight. His breath wafted the curls by her ear; his lips gently grazed her temple. Gently, so gently that she had no strength to resist, his hands lifted to her bare shoulders in a practised caress, skimming down over her bare arms. Ripples of delight shivered through her. He drew her around to face him, lifting one gloved hand and raising it to his lips.

"The evening is gone, sweetheart." His eyes lingered on hers, then dropped to her lips. For one instant, Georgiana wondered if he would kiss her. She hovered, poised on the brink of returning such an embrace, and felt oddly deflated when, in a voice curiously devoid of emotion, he remarked, "Come. Let me take you to find your party."

It was some minutes before Georgiana spied Arthur, Bella by his side, just inside the door to the main salon. She turned to the gentleman beside her, only to find he had disappeared, melting into the still considerable crowd. Suppressing a smile at his tactics, Georgiana went forward to Bella's side.

"Good heavens, Georgie! I was starting to wonder if you'd been spirited away." Bella looked closely at Georgiana, then asked, "Where have you been?"

"Oh, just here and there," replied Georgiana, smiling beatifically. She couldn't help her smile, even though it was making Bella suspicious. Still, with Arthur present, she doubted her friend would seek to interrogate her tonight. And she would handle tomorrow's queries when they came.

Ten minutes later, the Winsmere carriage rolled out along the road back to London.

Dominic Ridgeley watched it go. Pulling on his gloves, he nodded to a waiting footman, who promptly departed to summon the Viscount's carriage. Once comfortably ensconced in soft leather, the excellent springs ironing out the inevitable bumps and jolts, Dominic allowed his mind to coolly assess his involvement with Georgiana Hartley. He placed due emphasis on the "cool"; there had been more than one moment during the evening just past when, for all his experience, he had felt anything but cool. She was an enigma, his golden angel, an innocent who responded with delicious abandon to every practised caress he bestowed on her, who promised to respond with even greater passion to those caresses he had yet to expose her to. A golden angel who had already captured his hardened rake's heart, but, unless he mistook the matter, had yet to realise that fact. A fascinating proposition.

He treated the darkness to a smile of pure delight. Who would ever have believed it?

As the miles fell beneath his horses' hoofs, he relived the evening in his mind. She had accepted at face value his intimation that he hadn't recognised her. Would she still believe that tomorrow? And, if she did, what would she then make of his attentions to an unknown lady? Dominic grimaced. He would have to take the earliest opportunity to disabuse her mind of the idea he had not known who she was. Silly child. He would have known her instantly even if she had worn a full domino. Still, she did not have the experience to know she affected him as much as he affected her. More, if anything. The memory of how hard he had had to fight to refrain from kissing her on the terrace made him groan.

No more anonymous wooing. From now on, he resolved, he would openly court her. Doubtless, eyebrows would be raised. Too bad. His friends were sure to have recognised him tonight anyway. Julian Ellsmere certainly had. And Julian had known which lady he had spent the evening with. Thank heavens she had already refused Julian. The last thing he needed was to have a resurgence of the old story. God knew why the gossip-mongers had never realised that Julian himself bore him no ill will over the affair of Miss Amelia

Kerslake. His black brows rose cynically. Truth, of course, was never of great interest to the gossips.

With a deep sigh, Dominic leant back against the squabs and shut his eyes. Without the slightest difficulty, he conjured up the vision of a pair of big hazel eyes, so brilliant that they seemed to flash with gold fire. His doubts were gone. All considerations of age and station had long since fallen away, discarded as irrelevant in the face of his desire. He wanted Georgiana Hartley. And he intended to have her.

CHAPTER SIX

THE HATTRINGHAM HOUSE masked ball proved a revelation to others as well. While Georgiana waltzed and laughed on the arm of her cavalier, faded blue eyes, pale and washed out, watched her from the anonymity of the side of the room. Under his breath, Charles Hartley cursed. It didn't look promising.

Two weeks he had spent, searching the countryside for his little cousin. Finally he had been forced to conclude that the minx had somehow found her way to London. He had closed up the Place—had been forced to do so. Dismissing the Pringates had been an ugly affair, from which he was thankful to have escaped with a whole skin. But paying them off had severely depleted his reserves. He had hastened to town, reduced to finding lodgings in a mean and dingy street beyond the fashionable areas. Once installed, he had suddenly found himself at *point non plus*. Where would Georgie have gone?

That question had worried him until he was nearly crazed. Luckily, the recollection that her servants had disappeared with her surfaced to lead him from the brink of despair. From what he had seen of them, they would never have countenanced Georgiana doing anything that would bring her into danger. Or ill repute.

Hence, they must have found lodgings in an acceptable quarter.

Days of trudging the streets had followed, calling surreptitiously at the fashionable hotels, hours of drinking in the taverns favoured by the servants of the gentry. Gradually he had been forced to consider the more *tonnish* areas. Finally, his luck had turned. He had seen her in Bond Street.

She had been dressed in the height of fashion, a parasol shading her delicate features, and he had almost missed her. The effect her appearance had had on him, leaving him gaping, had, by sheer luck, saved him from prematurely revealing his presence.

Before he had gathered his wits, she was joined by another female, likewise fashionably elegant. A nagging sense of the familiar had finally crystallised. Little Bella Ridgeley! He had barely made her out, rigged up to the nines as she was, but she was still the little girl he had teased so unmercifully whenever her big brother had not been around.

His eyes had narrowed. So Georgiana had sought refuge at Candlewick Hall—the one place he had not considered looking. Smart of her—or was it pure luck? He had decided on luck, for there was no way Georgiana could have known, and was about to step forward and accost the fair pair, when they were helped into a waiting carriage by a burly footman.

Balked of his prey, the wisdom of reconnoitring the lie of the land was brought home to him. Bella had married a Lord Winsmere. A powerful man. If the Winsmeres were Georgiana's friends, he had better be sure of his strategy before he approached her.

He had followed the carriage through the bustling streets and had seen the ladies set down outside the house in Green Street. They had entered, and he had found an alley close by, from which he could keep the door in view. Georgiana had not re-emerged until the evening, when she had left in the carriage with Bella, both gorgeously arrayed in evening gowns. The sight of those gowns had sent a spasm of sheer fury through him. They had swanned off to a ball while he, half perished with cold, was forced to slink off to his miserable lodgings, with no prospect of a decent meal in sight. He had consoled himself with the thought that at least he now knew where his pigeon had come to roost.

But how to best approach the matter of getting his hands on her once more? With his limited resources, joining the social whirl was a near impossibility. His clothes alone would mark him as pecuniarily embarrassed. The cent per centers were too fly to be taken in by a glib tale; they would advance him nothing. Thanks to the restrictions his father's failings had placed on him, he had no friends among the swells. How to break into the glittering circle?

He had cudgelled his brains for hours. Eventually he had found a young tailor operating on the outskirts of the fashionable districts, one too inexperienced to quibble about his offer of a small down payment with the remainder of the costs to be sent on account. With his most immediate need assuaged, he had turned his mind to gaining an entrée to the balls and parties his cousin frequented.

The Hattringham House masked ball had presented

itself, ready-made for his needs. For the cost of a mask and a deal of studied self-confidence, he had been able to enter the ballroom as a guest, to wander slowly through the salons, carefully studying the female forms present. He had not even had to be covert about this enterprise; most of the young bucks were similarly engaged.

As it transpired, he had not recognised her. It was her voice, gaily answering some sally, which had identified her for him.

Now, as he watched her dance for the third time with the handsome dark-haired man who had monopolised her company for the entire evening, he ground his teeth. He stood no chance of competing honourably with the likes of her present cavalier. And, even from the obscurity of the sidelines, he could sense the rapport which existed between the pair. Damn her! She'd escaped him, only to fall victim to some other aspiring scoundrel. He brushed aside the thought that none but he knew her worth.

Seething, muttering imprecations beneath his breath, he watched helplessly as the dashing cavalier waltzed past, his cousin held securely in strong arms, mesmerised by a smile too experienced for any young damsel to resist.

"Soon," said Charles, entirely to himself. "I'll have to move soon." Having seen quite enough of his cousin and her consort to despair of parting them that night, he left Hattringham House, his brain awash with half-formed schemes.

IT WAS THE NEXT afternoon before Georgiana had leisure to thoroughly examine the events of the Hattringham House ball. Viewed in the calm light of day, she wasn't entirely sure what to make of them. Had he really not recognised her?

Over the weeks, by dint of subtle questioning, she had learnt a great deal more of Bella's brother. For instance, a quiet afternoon spent in the back parlour the previous week had yielded the tale of the initial incident that had given rise to Lord Alton's reputation of being dangerous company for young ladies.

"It happened during the Season immediately following Papa's death. Dominic had missed the beginning of the Season, still tied up with settling the estate." Bella had laid aside her embroidery and stared in concentration at the opposite wall. "I wasn't there, of course, but I've heard the tale umpteen times. Apparently Lord Ellsmere—he's a particular friend of Dominic's, you know—fell desperately in love with a scheming miss from somewhere up north. I forget her name—something like Kertlake. She and her mama had come to town determined to catch the biggest matrimonial prize." Bella turned to Georgiana. "Well, you know how eligible Julian Ellsmere is."

Georgiana had had the grace to look sheepish.

"Well," her preceptress had continued, "Julian fell very heavily, and no one could make him see what she was really like. Apparently she was an out-and-out schemer, flirting with every man, but carefully checking their assets at the same time. Lots of people tried to dissuade him, but he went ahead and proposed and was accepted. Then Dominic returned to town. He saw through Miss Whatever-her-name-was and de-

cided something had to be done. It was too late for
Julian to draw back with honour, so the lady had to
be made to withdraw." Bella had paused, eyeing
Georgiana carefully. Georgiana had raised her brows
in question. Bella had grimaced.

"You know what men are. And you've seen what
Dominic's like. So I don't suppose you'll find it hard
to believe that he swept the lady off her feet. He's a
bigger catch than Julian. So the lady broke off her
engagement with Julian, who by now had his eyes well
open. Dominic had managed it so she did it in the
expectation of him offering for her, but he never made
any formal declaration or anything like that. And, of
course, as soon as Julian was publicly free, Dominic
just dumped the girl. The trouble was, not everyone
was in the know. A lot of gossips just saw Dominic
entrapping a beautiful girl and then ruthlessly discard-
ing her. That's what started it all. And, needless to
say, Dominic doesn't give a damn what people think
of him. Naturally, all his friends know the truth."

At this point, Bella had picked up her embroidery
again. Then she had paused, to add matter-of-factly,
"Of course, later, when he went around seducing all
the bored wives and beautiful widows—the Lady
Changleys of the world, you understand—they simply
painted his reputation blacker."

Smothering a choking laugh, Georgiana had bent
her head once more over her own embroidery, her
thoughts far removed from *petit point*.

"Mind you," Bella had added, waving her needle
in the air to give her point emphasis, "despite all, he's
never particularly enamoured of them—the women he

seduces, I mean." She had frowned, totally absorbed in her subject and no longer conscious of her audience. "I suspect it's because it's all so easy." She had shrugged. "Just like me, getting bored with the Season—it's all too easy without some purpose behind it."

They had fallen silent after that, each busy with their own thoughts.

Now Georgiana sat alone in the back parlour, having seen Bella off on a visit to her old nurse. Her thoughts revolved incessantly, driven by an unnerving juxtaposition of longing and uncertainty. The breathtaking thrill of basking in the warmth of his smouldering blue gaze... All the subtle attentions he had paid her throughout the long night of the masked ball... She'd already lost her heart to Lord Alton. Now he seemed intent on leading her on to more dangerous ground. But had he known it was her he was leading? Surely not. Her mind rebelled at the thought. If he had known, then that would mean... No. He couldn't be seriously pursuing her. What on earth could he mean by it, if he was? And what on earth was she to do about it?

She puzzled and worried at her questions, but when Johnson knocked and entered the room two hours later she had still not found any answer.

"There's a gentleman to see you, miss. A Mr Charles Hartley."

The butler's words effectively banished Georgiana's dreams. Charles? Here? How on earth had he traced her? And why?

The soft clearing of Johnson's throat recalled her

scattered wits. She had enough unanswerable questions without Charles adding to the score. And, secure and safe in Winsmere House, she had no reason to fear her cousin. Johnson, she felt sure, would hover protectively near the door. "My cousin?" It was hard to believe.

Johnson bowed. "The gentleman did mention the connection, miss."

From the butler's stiff tone, Georgiana surmised her cousin had failed to find favour in his shrewd eyes. The observation gave her confidence. "I'll see him in here."

"Very good, miss." Johnson made for the door, but paused with his hand on the knob. "I'll be just outside the door, miss, in case you should need anything."

Georgiana smiled her gratitude as Johnson withdrew.

A minute later, the door opened once more to allow Charles Hartley to enter. In the light streaming in through the long windows, Georgiana studied her cousin as he crossed the room towards her. His appearance had improved considerably since last they had met. She suppressed a grin at the memory. He had been drunk. Now he was clearly quite sober. His clothes were not as elegant as those she had grown used to seeing, but were clean and, unless she much mistook the matter, new. His cravat was tied neatly, if not with flair. A great improvement over the stained and ill fitting togs he had worn at the Place. He was neither tall nor short, neither corpulent nor lanky. Yet his figure was unimpressive compared to the other in her mind. His colouring was much paler and less vibrant than her own. Lank fair hair hung across pallid skin; pale reptilian eyes regarded her with little evidence of emotion. Repressing her instinctive shrinking, she extended her hand as he drew near. "Charles."

As he took her hand and bowed over it, Charles was conscious that his little cousin had somehow changed. The young girl who had fled to her chamber to escape his lovemaking had grown even more lovely. And more confident. But she would never be a match for him. He smiled, struggling to keep his thoughts from showing. She had blossomed into a more delectable piece than he would have predicted. The figure outlined by the bronze silk dress she had worn at the ball was quite real, albeit now garbed in sober grey. Perhaps he would enjoy the role of her husband rather more than he had anticipated.

At his continued scrutiny, Georgiana allowed her brows to rise haughtily.

Recalled to his purpose, Charles assumed a serious face. "Georgiana, I've come to beg your pardon."

Now Georgiana's brows flew upwards in surprise.

Charles smiled tentatively and pressed his advantage. "For my boorish behaviour at the Place. I... Well—" he shrugged and smiled self-deprecatingly "—I was swept away with desire, my dear. I should have told you, of course, of the arrangements that had been made. But I had a hope you would love me for myself and it would not be necessary. I see now I should have explained it to you at the start. You see, my father and your father wanted us to marry." At her instinctive recoil, Charles raised a placating hand.

"Oh, at first I felt as you. You can imagine my dismay, a young man being told his marriage was already arranged. I ranted and raved, but in the end I agreed to do my duty to the family. So I waited for the day your father would send you home. As things fell out, he died before he had brought himself to tell you and send you away from him." Pale eyes carefully scrutinised Georgiana's face. "I can imagine how attached he was to you, and doubtless he sought to keep you by him for as long as possible." Charles smiled meaningfully into Georgiana's eyes. "I can understand his feelings."

To his consternation, Charles could detect no response to his revelations, other than a slight widening of the huge hazel eyes.

"In the circumstances, you can imagine my surprise when I first saw you, first learned of your beauty."

Another smile accompanied this piece of flattery, but evoked no hint of feminine preening.

Charles frowned. Was the child paying attention? He turned the frown to good effect as he continued, "I'm afraid my behaviour was rather wild. I can only ask you to excuse my excesses on the grounds of my incredible relief that, now you were finally here, everything was going to be all right."

Still Georgiana gave no sign of reaction to his tale.

Mentally groping in the dark, Charles put on a humble face and asked, "Georgiana, can you possibly forgive me?"

At the start of her cousin's tale, Georgiana had schooled her features to impassivity. As his story unfurled, she was thankful for the iron control, polished over the weeks of social gadding, that held her silent. She had no doubt that the existence of a long-standing, family-arranged betrothal between them was a fabrication. Her father had always shown particular concern for her eventual state. He had not expected to die suddenly, it was true. But that he had died forgetting to tell her she was formally betrothed was impossible. She resisted the impulse to laugh scornfully, and forced her voice to a cool and even tone. "I suggest your behaviour at the Place is best forgotten."

At his too ready smile, she assumed her most regal manner and forged on. "However, as to this other matter you have raised, of us being betrothed, I'm afraid I must insist that such a betrothal never occurred. Certainly my father never told me of it. Nor were there any documents among his effects to support such a notion. I'm afraid, if your father led you to suppose there was an agreement, then he misled you."

Charles's frown was quite genuine. So much for that idea. He would have to try his second string. He turned slightly and moved away from his cousin, taking a few steps away, then pacing back. His features obediently fell into a look of downcast dismay. He looked straight at Georgiana, an expression of wordless misery on his face. Then he gestured eloquently and turned aside. "Georgiana. My dear, what can I say to convince you?"

If she had not been so sensitive on the subject, Georgiana would have found his histrionics quite entertaining. As it was, she felt no inclination to smile, let alone laugh.

From the corner of his eye, Charles watched her

stony countenance. Intuition told him an avowal of love would fall on barren soil. Instead, he opted for a more avuncular line. "I would do everything possible to make you happy. Your father's death has left you alone in the world. Please, I beg you, allow me to take on the task of caring for you."

Georgiana barely managed to keep from laughing in his face. He, to talk of caring for her! He had threatened her—more than threatened her—and under his own roof! She could manage quite well, she felt, without his sort of protection. With perfect composure she replied, "Please say no more. My mind is quite unalterable on this point. I will not marry you, Charles."

Yet another proposal, she thought with a wry inward grin. Even less welcome than the others.

Charles sighed dramatically and turned so she could no longer see his face. All in all, he was just as well suited with her decision. It was hardly a great surprise. At least now he had a clear path to follow. After a pained moment, he turned back to her and smiled bravely. "I knew it was no use. But, you see, I felt I had to try. If I could just ask that we remain friends?"

Georgiana blinked. Friends? Well, it couldn't hurt to make that concession. It meant so little. She smiled gently, somewhat relieved that the episode seemed set to conclude on a much more reasonable note than she had anticipated. She held out her hand, a friendly enough gesture, but still a clear dismissal. "Friends, then, if you wish it."

Charles took her hand and bowed over it. As he straightened, his face cleared as if reminded of a pleasant event. "Ah, I nearly forgot." His eyes sought

Georgiana's. "Those paintings you were looking for. At the Place."

Georgiana's heart leapt.

Sensing her response, Charles inwardly smirked. So much for her impenetrable shell.

"Yes?" Georgiana prompted, not bothering to conceal her eagerness.

Charles smiled. "I don't want to get your hopes up, but the Pringates were clearing out the attics when I left. They sent me a message two days ago that they had found some pictures, among other things. I wrote back to ask who had painted them. If they are the ones you seek…" He let his voice trail away.

Breathlessly Georgiana seized the proffered moment to issue the invitation Charles was angling for. "You'll let me know at once? Please, Charles?"

Genuinely pleased, he allowed his smile to broaden. "I'll let you know at once."

Deeming it wise to leave well enough alone, he merely bowed over her hand and smiled encouragingly as she crossed to the bell-pull to summon the butler.

NATURALLY, after she had considered the matter from all angles, Georgiana sought Bella's opinion of Charles's visit and his declaration.

"*Friends?*" The incredulity in Bella's voice left little doubt of her opinion of Charles. She snorted. "He's a bounder. Always was, always will be."

Georgiana shrugged. "Well, that's neither here nor there." She bent her head over her stitchery. It was the day after Charles's visit and they were in the back parlour, as was their habit of a morning.

Bella stifled a yawn. "Ye gods! I declare I'm infected with your illness."

Georgiana raised an enquiring eyebrow.

"Finding the evenings over-tiring," Bella explained. "I would never have thought a musical supper would be so positively exhausting."

"I rather think that depends on the music," put in Georgiana, with a smile for her hostess. "Besides, from what I saw, you were half asleep through most of the recital."

Bella waved a hand airily. "It's fashionable to nod off. All the best people do it."

With a gurgle of laughter, Georgiana set her work aside. "Seriously, though, do you think Charles will give me my father's paintings back?"

"Don't get too carried away. They might not be your father's at all."

A discreet knock heralded Johnson's entry. "A note for you, miss. There's a messenger waiting for your reply."

Georgiana lifted the simple note from Johnson's salver. It was sealed with a nondescript lump of wax.

Dismissing her butler with a nod, Bella turned to find her friend regarding the missive in her hand with some nervousness. "Well? Open it!"

With a small sigh, Georgiana broke the seal and spread out the single sheet. "It's from Charles," she told the waiting Bella. After a moment, her face brightened. "He's found them! Oh, Bella! They were there after all!"

Seeing the sunshine in Georgiana's face, Bella relaxed and grinned back. "How lovely for you. Is he sending them over?"

Georgiana was reading on. A small frown clouded her brow, then lifted. "Yes and no. He hasn't actually got them yet. He says he's sent to Pringate to bring them to the Hart and Hounds—that's the posting inn, the last before London on the road to Candlewick. I remember stopping there on our way here."

Bella nodded absent-mindedly. "Yes, but why? Why not just bring them to London?"

Georgiana, engrossed in deciphering Charles's scrawl, shrugged aside the quibble. "Charles says he's going to meet Pringate this afternoon to pick up the pictures, and asks if I would like to come too. Oh, Bella! Just think! By this afternoon I'll have them."

"Mmm." Bella eyed her friend with a frown. It would be of no use to tell Georgiana that Charles was not to be trusted. From her face it was clear nothing on earth would stop her from going to fetch her paintings. With a definite feeling of misgiving, Bella held her peace.

While Georgiana penned an enthusiastic reply to Charles's invitation, Bella sat and worriedly chewed her lip. But, by the time Johnson departed to give Georgiana's note to the messenger, she had perked up and was able to listen to Georgiana's excited ramblings with an indulgent smile. It was obvious really. To protect Georgiana from Charles's machinations, all she had to do was precisely what she had always done whenever Charles had threatened. She would tell Dominic.

When Charles called for Georgiana at three, Bella

played least in sight. Charles was high on her list of unfavourite people. She had already surreptitiously dispatched a note to her brother, summoning him to her instant aid. As she watched Charles's small phaeton carry Georgiana away, she struggled to subdue a disturbing sense of disquiet.

Impatiently, she waited for Dominic to call.

ENSCONCED in the comfort of well padded leather, Dominic Ridgeley, Lord Ridgeley, Viscount Alton, man of the world and political intriguer, was deep in consideration of the beauties of nature. Or, more specifically, one particular golden-haired, golden-eyed beauty. The silence of the reading room of White's was punctuated by the occasional snore and snuffle and the crackle of turning pages. Otherwise, there was no sound to distract him from his reverie. The daily news-sheet was held open before his face, but he would have been hard pressed to recall the headlines, let alone the substance of any of the articles. This morning Georgiana Hartley occupied his mind to the exclusion of all else.

He had not seen her for over twenty-four hours. Which fact, he felt, was more than ample excuse for his preoccupation. A political dinner had prevented him from attending Lady Overington's musical supper—a mixed blessing, he was sure. Hence, he had to be content with reliving the events of the masked ball. A slow grin twisted his lips as he recalled his angel's response to some of his more outrageous sallies. He would have to make certain he disabused her mind of her apparent belief that he had not known her identity.

The point niggled, like a burr caught under his collar. It had been a strategic error, to allow her to leave him still thinking he was showering his attentions on a damsel unknown to him. An error he was more than experienced enough to recognise. Still, he would ensure the matter was rectified at their next meeting— tonight, at the Pevenseys' gala. Consideration of her likely reactions to his revelations kept him entertained for some minutes. The sight of her face when the penny finally dropped, her innocent confusion, all unknowingly reflected in her glorious eyes, would afford him untold pleasure.

A soft smile of pure anticipation curved his fine lips.

Seeing it, Lord Ellsmere paused, before clearing his throat meaningfully.

At the sound so close by his ear, Dominic jumped. His eyes met those of his friend in pained surprise.

Julian Ellsmere grinned. "Interesting thoughts, old man?"

Dominic struggled up out of the depths of his chair. "Damn you, Julian! I was just—"

"Shhhh!" came hissing from all corners of the room.

"Come into the smoking-room," whispered Lord Ellsmere. "I've got some news I think you should hear."

They had been at Eton, then Oxford, together, had shared all the larks and adventures of well heeled young men. And had remained close friends to the present. Which, when they'd found a secluded corner of the smoking-room, allowed Lord Ellsmere to say, "Don't know how deep your interest goes with your sister's protégée, but I just saw her being driven out of town by a rather rum customer. Tow-headed, pasty-faced bounder.''

The sudden hardening of the lines of his friend's face told Lord Ellsmere more clearly than words just how deeply Dominic Ridgeley's interest in Georgiana Hartley went.

''When?''

'''Bout twenty minutes. Up the North Road.''

Dominic's eyes had narrowed. ''Tow-headed?'' When Julian Ellsmere nodded, he continued, ''Medium height and build? Fair skin?''

''That's the man. Know him?''

But Dominic was muttering curses under his breath and heading for the door. When Julian caught him up in the hall, where the porter was scurrying to find his cane and gloves, Dominic turned to him and said, ''My thanks.''

Lord Ellsmere waved one languid hand. ''Oh, think nothing of it. As I recall, I owe you one.'' He smiled, then sobered to ask, ''You'll go after her?''

''Most assuredly. The silly chit should have known better. I'd go bail that's her cousin she's with. And between Charles Hartley and a viper there's not much difference.''

The porter returned, and Dominic pulled on his gloves. As he took his cane from the man, Lord Ellsmere, frowning, added, ''One other thing. Might be significant. This tow-headed chap... Saw him leaving Hattringham House t'other night.''

The chill in Dominic's eyes was pronounced. ''You're sure?''

Julian Ellsmere nodded. "Quite certain." After a moment he asked, "Need any help?"

At that, Dominic smiled in a way that made Julian Ellsmere feel almost sorry for Charles Hartley. "No. I've dealt with Charles before. It'll be a particular pleasure to make it clear to him that Miss Hartley is very definitely out of bounds."

Lord Ellsmere nodded and clapped his friend on the shoulder.

With a fleeting smile, Dominic was gone.

A brisk walk saw him entering Alton House. Immediately the door shut behind him, he issued a string of commands which had his groom and coachman running to the mews and his valet pounding up the stairs in search of his greatcoat.

Dominic waited in the hall, frowning, his cane, still in his hand, tapping impatiently against one booted foot. Julian had said he had seen them. That meant an open carriage. Surely Charles wasn't proposing to drive her all the way to Buckinghamshire in an open carriage? No. When dusk fell, the cold would be intense. Presumably the open carriage was just part of his scheme, whatever that was.

Timms's cough interrupted his thoughts. "I don't know as this is the most opportune moment, m'lord, but this note came some time ago from Lady Winsmere."

Dominic's frown lifted. He took the note and broke it open. The sound of his carriage drawing up in the street coincided with his man's precipitate descent with his coat. An instant later, garbed in his many caped greatcoat and clutching his sisters missive in his hand, Viscount Alton climbed into his carriage.

"Winsmere House. Quickly!"

"OH, DOMINIC! Thank God you've come. I've been so worried." Bella's plaintive wail greeted Dominic as he crossed the threshold of her parlour.

"Don't fly into a pucker, Bella. Julian Ellsmere has just told me he saw Georgiana leaving town with a man who sounds like Charles. Has she?"

"Yes!" Bella was wringing her hands in agitation. "She was so set on it, I knew I couldn't stop her. But I don't trust Charles one inch. That's why I sent for you."

Taking note of his sister's unusually pale face, Dominic replied with far greater calmness than he felt. "Quite right." He swallowed his impatience and smiled reassuringly. "Why don't we sit down and you can tell me all about it?"

Haltingly, prodded by gentle questions, the tale of Charles's visit and the subsquent events was retold. By the end of the tale, Dominic was confident he saw the light. He leant forward to pat Bella's hand. "Don't worry. I'll fetch her back."

Bella blinked up at him as he stood. "You'll go straight away?"

"I was setting out when Timms gave me your note. Just as well. At least now I can go directly to the Hare and Hounds." Dominic's blue eyes critically surveyed his sister. At his insistence she reclined on the *chaise*. Her face was too pale and her agitation was too marked, even given the cause. Shrewdly he drew his own conclusions. He had been going to suggest she come with him, to lend propriety to their return to Green Street. But in her present condition he rather thought any further excitement was to be assiduously avoided. And, if truth be known, he would much rather be alone with Georgiana on the drive back to town. He had every intention of reading her a lecture on the subject of herself—care of. Afterwards, he felt sure he would enjoy her attempts to be conciliatory, not to mention grateful. And it would give him a heaven-sent opportunity to correct her mistaken assumption regarding his conduct at the masked ball. Yes, he was definitely looking forward to the return journey. Propriety, in this instance, could go hang.

He smiled again at his sister. ''Don't fret. Arthur will be home shortly. You can tell him all about it. I suspect we won't make it back until late, so you'd best send your regrets to the Pevenseys.''

''Lord, yes! I couldn't face a party on top of all this.''

Dominic grinned, then bent to bestow a kiss on one pale cheek. ''Take care, my dear. You burn the candle with a vengeance.''

She grimaced at him but refused to rise to the bait.

Dominic crossed the room, but turned at the door to consider the listless figure on the *chaise*. Had she realised yet herself? One dark brow rose. With a last affectionate smile, he left.

CHAPTER SEVEN

JOYFUL ANTICIPATION of seeing her mother's face again carried Georgiana through the streets of London, unaware of the man beside her. However, as the phaeton turned northwards and the more populated streets fell behind, a tingling sense of premonition awoke in her mind.

The afternoon remained fine, a brisk breeze whipping at her cloak and bonnet, promising hard frosts for the morning. As the buildings thinned, the air became perceptibly chillier. Charles's conversation, uninspiring though it had been, had disappeared along with the fashionable dwellings. He seemed to be concentrating on driving the carriage at a slow but steady pace.

Georgiana stared ahead, willing the comforting bulk of the Hare and Hounds to loom on the horizon. But, from Green Street, it would take at least an hour to reach the comfort of the posting inn. A frown drew the golden arches of her brows together. Charles had called for her at three, which, now she came to think more clearly, was surely a little late for an expedition of such distance. It would be dark by the time they returned to Winsmere House. Still, there was little she could do about it now, beyond praying that the plodding nag drawing the phaeton would find its second wind. With a discontented grimace, she gave her attention to their surroundings. She refused to give further consideration to the doubt nagging from the deepest recesses of her mind, the little voice which warned that something was amiss.

Ten minutes later, a surreptitious movement beside her had her turning her head in time to see Charles replace his fob watch in his pocket.

He smiled at her. ''Not long now.''

Georgiana knew the smile was meant to reassure. It missed its mark. Odd how she had forgotten how Charles's smiles so rarely reached his eyes. Her suspicions, unspecified but now fully awakened, took possession of her mind. The horse's plodding hoofs beat a slow accompaniment to her increasingly trepidatious heartbeat as she reviewed the potential threats she might all too soon have to face.

In the end, she was so preoccupied with her imaginary dragons that she missed the sight of the Hare and Hounds. Only when Charles turned the phaeton under the arch of the innyard did she shake off her reverie to look about her.

She had stopped here on her way to London. But that time she had been travelling in the luxury of Lord Alton's coach, with attentive servants to guard her. Now, as Charles handed her down from the open carriage, she glanced about to see the yard full of people. Ostlers hurried fresh horses out of the stables beyond the yard, while others led weary equines freed of the traces to rest. Stableboys rushed hither and yon, under everyone's feet, helping with the harness and carrying baggage back and forth from the inn. Inn servants stood with jugs of steaming ale and mulled wine, ready to refresh the passengers of the coaches pulled up for the change of horses. At the centre of the commotion stood the southbound accommodation coach, a huge, ponderous vehicle, settled like a dull black bullfrog on the cobbles. The passengers were alighting for their evening meal. Georgiana found herself the object of not a few staring eyes. She was about to turn away when one gentleman raised his high-crowned beaver and bowed.

With a start, Georgiana recognised a distant acquaintance of Bella's and Arthur's. She had been introduced to him at one of the balls. With a small smile, she acknowledged the bow, wondering at the hardlipped, cold-eyed look the man gave her.

Accepting Charles's arm over the uneven surface, more from necessity than inclination, she was about to ascend the two steps to the inn's main door when a sudden commotion on the coach's roof claimed all eyes. Three well dressed youths—roof passengers— were laughingly struggling with each other. At the coachman's loud "Hoi!", they desisted and, shame-facedly realising they were the centre of attention, sought to descend to less exalted positions. Waiting for his companions to climb down the rungs before him, one of the young men looked about the yard and caught sight of Georgiana. Her eyes met his with a jolt of recognition. He was the younger brother of one of the débutantes being presented that Season. She had danced with him at his sister's come-out. His open-mouth stare told Georgiana quite clearly that something was severely wrong.

She had barely time to smile at the young man before Charles tugged her through the inn door. To her surprise, she found that Charles had hired a private parlour for their use. Distracted by the memory of the stares of the two gentlemen in the yard, she paid scant attention to this discovery. As she meekly followed the innkeeper up the wooden staircase, the reason for the stares occurred. Of course! She and Charles shared no more than a fleeting family resemblance. The gentlemen thought she was here, alone, with a man who was no relation. She blushed slightly. There was, of course, nothing wrong with being escorted somewhere by one's cousin. She knew that. It was often the case in Italy, where families were large. She had not thought there was any impropriety attached to her going to an inn with Charles. Surely, if there had been, Bella would have raised some demur? But the disapprobation on the older man's face, and the sheer stunned disbelief in the younger's, stayed with her, banishing all ease.

So, when she heard the click from the parlour door as the latch fell into place behind the burly innkeeper, it was with a heightened sense of suspicion that she surveyed the neat parlour. It was empty. No Pringates. No paintings. Georgiana's heart plummeted. Drawing a steadying breath, she turned to face Charles. "Where are the Pringates?"

Her cousin stood, leaning against the door, watching her with a shrewdly calculating gaze. After a moment, he pushed away from the solid oak panels and strolled towards her. "Doubtless they've been delayed. Let me take your cloak."

Automatically surrendering her cloak, Georgiana forcibly repressed a shudder as Charles's fingers inadvertently brushed her shoulders in removing it. Inadvertently? She risked a quick glance up at his face. What she saw there did nothing for her peace of mind. Quelling the panic rising within, she forced herself to act ingenuously. "Are we going to wait for them?"

Charles straightened from laying her cloak over a chair. Again she was subjected to a careful scrutiny. Georgiana struggled to quieten the hammering of her nerves and face him calmly. Apparently Charles was satisfied with what he saw.

"Having come this far, we might as well wait for a while." His eyes raked her face again. "Perhaps a tea tray would fill in the time?"

Eager to have something to occupy them ostensibly while she considered the ramifications of her latest impulsive start, Georgiana forced a smile of agreement to her lips.

The innkeeper was summoned and, in short order, a buxom young serving girl bustled in with a tray loaded with teapot, scones and all necessary appurtenances. Charles dismissed her with a nod and a coin, holding the door for her.

Under cover of wielding the teapot, Georgiana watched Charles close the door. She almost sighed audibly when she saw he did not bother to lock it.

With renewed confidence, fragile though she suspected it was, she gave her mind over to plotting her moves. The first imperative was to learn what Charles had in mind. And, she supposed, there was always the possibility that she was inventing horrors where none existed. A slim hope, she felt, with her nerves jangling in insistent warning.

Taking a sip of strong tea to help steady herself, she asked, "There are no paintings, are there?"

Her question coincided with Charles taking a sip from his own cup. He choked but recovered swiftly. His faded blue gaze lifted and fixed on her face, and she had her answer. He smiled, not pleasantly. Georgiana felt her muscles tense.

"How perceptive of you, sweet cousin."

His congratulatory tone purred sarcastically in her ears. For the first time since leaving the Place, Georgiana knew she was face-to-face with the real Charles Hartley. She fought down a wild desire to rush to the door. Charles might not be large, but he was a great deal larger than she was. Besides, she needed to know more. She was sick of mysteries. "Why? Why all this elaborate charade? What do you hope to gain?"

Charles laughed mirthlessly, his eyes never leaving her face. "What I want. Your hand in marriage." Then his gaze slid slowly over her. "Among other things."

His tone made Georgiana feel physically ill. She forced herself to sip her tea calmly, drawing what strength she could from the strong black brew. Her mind wandered frantically amid the pieces of the puzzle but could not make out the picture.

"Not worked it out yet?"

Charles's taunt broke into her mental meanderings. She looked at him coldly.

He smiled, enjoying her obvious discomfort. He

leant back in his chair, balancing it on its back legs. "I'll spell it out for you, if you like."

Georgiana decided that, however distressful, knowing his plans had to be her primary aim. So she allowed a look of patent interest to infuse her features.

Charles's lips twisted in a gloating grin. "My plan is quite simple. We arrived here just as the accommodation coach was unloading. You were seen entering this inn with me by at least two people who know you. That, in itself, will cause only minor comment. However, when we leave here tomorrow morning, while the northbound accommodation coach passengers are breakfasting in the main room downstairs, I feel certain the sight of you leaving at such an early hour with me, without the benefit of maid or baggage, is going to raise quite a few brows."

Georgiana's heart sank as she pictured the scene. He was right, of course. Even she knew what a scandal such a sighting would provoke, regardless of the truth of the matter.

"So, you see, after that you'll have little choice but to accept my proposal." Charles's grin turned decidedly wicked.

Georgiana had had enough. Carefully replacing her cup on the tray, she wiped her hands on the napkin and then, laying the cloth aside, fixed her cousin with a determined stare. "Charles, I have no idea why you are so set on marrying me. You don't even like me."

At that, he laughed. Hand over heart, he bowed from the waist mockingly. "I assure you, sweet Georgie, I'll manage to drum up enough enthusiasm to convince all and sundry of what took place here."

Georgiana shook her head slowly. "It won't work, you know. I won't marry you. There's no reason why I should."

The cynical twist of Charles's lips told her she had not heard all of his plan. "I hesitate to correct you, fair cousin, but, unless you want the Winsmeres mired in scandal, you'll most certainly marry me. It won't have escaped the notice of the gossip-mongers that you're supposedly in their care."

Involuntarily, Georgiana's lip curled. "You really are despicable, you know."

To her surprise, her tone was perfectly controlled. In fact she felt strangely calm. The lack of expression in Charles's cold eyes sent shivers up and down her spine. But now her own, usually latent temper was on the rise. It had been one thing when he had threatened *her;* to threaten her friends was another matter entirely. She folded her hands and met his gaze unflinchingly. "Be that as it may, I repeat, I will not marry you. Unless things have changed rather dramatically in England, I suspect you still need me to speak my vows. That being so, if you persist in your plan to ruin my reputation, then, when I leave here, I will stop at Green Street only long enough to pick up my luggage and servants. I'll return to Ravello." Summoning a disaffected shrug, she lifted her chin and added, "I always meant to go back eventually. And, with me gone, no scandal of any magnitude will touch Bella and Arthur."

For one long moment, Charles stared at her, eyes quite blank. It had never occurred to him, when he had planned this little campaign, that his prey would simply refuse to co-operate. Having seen her riding high in the social whirl, the threat of a catastrophic fall from grace had seemed an unbeatable card. Now, looking into hazel eyes that held far too much calmness, Charles knew he was facing defeat. Typically, he chose to counter with the usual threat of a bully. With a low growl, he rose menacingly, his chair falling back with a clatter on the floor.

Georgiana's eyes widened in dismay. She felt trapped, unable to move, caught and transfixed by the animosity which poured from Charles's eyes. Not until then had she realised just how much he disliked—nay, hated—her. She stopped breathing.

Charles was poised to come around the table, muscles tensed to lay ungentle hands on her, when the unlikely sound of quiet applause broke across Georgiana's strained senses. She turned towards the door.

Deafened by his anger, Charles only turned after seeing her attention distracted.

The sight that met their eyes was, to Georgiana, as welcome as it was unbelievable. The door lay open. Absorbed in their mutual revelations, neither had heard the click of the latch. Leaning against the doorframe, his greatcoat open and negligently thrown over his shoulders to reveal the elegance of his attire, Lord Alton surveyed the room. Having successfully gained the attention of both its occupants, he smiled at Georgiana and, pushing away from the door, strolled towards her.

In a daze, Georgiana stood and held out her hand, bemused by the sudden turn of events. Blue eyes met hers, conveying warming reassurance and something else—something very like irritation. Bewildered, Georgiana blinked.

Dominic took her hand and bowed over it, then placed it on his arm and covered it comfortingly with his own large hand. "Miss Hartley. I am here, as arranged, to convey you back to town."

Georgiana's eyes flew to his and read the silent message there. The warmth of his hand banished her fears. She had complete confidence in him.

With an encouraging smile, Dominic turned and, seeing her cloak, released her to fetch it.

The action broke the spell which had held Charles immobile. His normal pasty complexion had paled at the sight of his childhood nemesis. Now his face flooded with unbecoming colour. "You're out of order, Ridgeley," he ground out through clenched teeth. "My cousin is in my care. And she's not returning to London."

Settling Georgiana's cloak about her shoulders, Dominic raised his brows in fascinated contemplation of the thinly veiled threat. His gaze met Charles's squarely, then wandered insultingly over the younger man's frame. Dominic Ridgeley was a man in his prime, a noted Corinthian, five years older, three inches taller and two stone of sheer muscle heavier than Charles Hartley. And Charles knew it.

To Georgiana's intense relief, he dropped his eyes, blanching, then flushing again. Bella's brother tucked her hand in the crook of his arm and patted it comfortingly.

"Come, my dear. My carriage is waiting."

By some magical machination, Georgiana found

herself escorted gently but firmly out of the inn by a route which exposed her to no one other than the inn-keeper, bowing obsequiously as they passed. Handed into the same luxuriously appointed coach that she had used on her previous visit to the inn, she sank back against the fine leather with a small sigh of relief tinged with disillusionment. The search for her mother's portrait had nearly ended in nightmare.

The evening was closing in. Georgiana glanced up to see Lord Alton's large frame silhouetted by the light thrown by the flares in the innyard. He paused, one foot on the carriage step, and gazed back at the inn, an expression she could not define on his face. Then, abruptly, he stepped back. "Your pardon, my dear. Unfinished business." He frowned and added, "I won't keep you more than a minute."

He shut the carriage door, and Georgiana heard him call up to the coachman to watch over her. Peering out of the window, she saw him stride purposefully through the main door of the inn.

As the minutes ticked by, the conviction grew that Lord Alton's "unfinished business" lay with Charles. Georgiana fretted, frustrated by her helplessness. She had almost reached the point of sending the coachman in search of his master when Lord Alton appeared on the inn steps. As he strode across the yard, Georgiana scanned his person. He was undeniably intact. His greatcoat swung, impeccable as ever, from his broad shoulders. She expelled a little sigh of pent-up breath and hurriedly moved farther along the seat to make room for her rescuer. Then he was in the carriage and they were moving.

To her consternation, Georgiana found travelling in a closed carriage with Bella's brother was almost as much as an ordeal as being in the inn parlour with Charles. But, while with Charles she'd had to subdue her disgust, with Lord Alton it was an entirely different emotion she fought to control. At one level, she revelled in his nearness, in the delicate wafts of sandalwood and leather that subtly teased her senses. Occasionally a deep rut jolted her shoulder against his arm. But the feelings which rose up inside her were too dangerous, too damning. Ruthlessly, she fought to quell them, forcing her breathing to slow and her mind to function.

"Did Bella send you?"

Dominic had been waiting, with what patience he could muster, for her to recover. He frowned into the gathering gloom and turned towards her. "Both Bella *and* Julian Ellsmere."

"Lord Ellsmere?"

"The same. He saw you leaving London with Charles—a 'tow-headed bounder' was his description."

His clipped tones destroyed any impulse Georgiana had to laugh.

"Then Bella sent around a note and told me where to look for you." Dominic studied his angel's face in the faint glow of light cast back from the carriage lamps. He could see no sign that she understood the danger she had been in, no comprehension of the fear and worry her impulsive start had visited on him. His tone became noticeably drier. "I find it hard to understand why, knowing Charles as you do, you consented to this ill advised junket.''

At the clear censure in his voice, Georgiana stiffened. She swallowed the peculiar lump in her throat to say in a small, tight voice, ''I'm sorry if I've caused you any inconvenience.''

Inwardly Dominic cursed. This interlude was not progressing as planned. He was having the devil of a time holding on to his temper, rubbed raw by the troubled speculation of the hour and more it had taken to reach the inn. The impulse to shake her was strong. Yet, in his present mood, he doubted the wisdom of laying hands on her. And, wise in the ways of young ladies, he knew his angel, far from being adoringly penitent, was close to taking snuff. If he gave in to temptation and read her the lecture burning the tip of his tongue, she might well treat him to a deplorable display of feminine weakness. For once, he wasn't sure of his ability to withstand such a scene. With a ''Humph!'', he folded his arms across his chest and stared moodily out of the window.

For her part, Georgiana kept her gaze firmly fixed on the passing shadows, concentrating on subduing her quivering lips and blinking away the sudden moisture in her large eyes. It was really too much! First he had taken charge of her, like a guardian, just because she had asked for help. Then he had not had the sense to recognise her at the masked ball and had made her lose her heart with his wickedly sophisticated ways. Now he was treating her like a child again, upbraiding her, blaming *her* instead of Charles!

Trying not to sniff, Georgiana determinedly dragged